Praise for *Major Gift*

"A treat for the soul. Ezuma navigates a beautiful exploration of grief and self-worth dappled with the shiny sparks of new love."

—Christine Riccio, *New York Times* bestselling author of *Again, but Better* and *Attached at the Hip*

Major Gift

TIFFANY EZUMA

831 STORIES

831 Stories

An imprint of Authors Equity
1123 Broadway, Suite 1008
New York, New York 10010

Copyright © 2026 by Tiffany Ezuma
All rights reserved.

Cover design by C47
Book design by Scribe Inc.

This is a work of fiction. Names, characters, places and incidents either are products of the author's imagination or are used fictitiously.

Most Authors Equity books are available at a discount when purchased in quantity for sales promotions or corporate use. Special editions, which include personalized covers, excerpts, and corporate imprints, can be created when purchased in large quantities. For more information, please email info@authorsequity.com.

No part of this publication may be reproduced, distributed, or transmitted in any form or by any means, including photocopying, recording, other electronic or mechanical methods, or for the purpose of training artificial intelligence technologies or systems, without the prior written permission of the publisher, except in the case of noncommercial uses permitted by copyright law.

Library of Congress Control Number: 2026931309
Print ISBN 9798893311426
Ebook ISBN 9798893311440

Printed in the United States of America
First printing

www.831stories.com
www.authorsequity.com

To my father,
who gives me the courage to keep creating

PROLOGUE

London, England

My lungs are burning. I don't know why I do this to myself every morning.

I keep swimming back and forth across the pool despite every atom in my body begging me to stop.

I'm not a natural swimmer. I only learned how ten months ago, when Robyn, my grief counselor, suggested exercise might help me cope. After trying everything from Pilates to boxing, swimming was the only thing that stuck. There's something about the repetition, the simple task of putting one arm in front of the other, that forces my mind to focus. That is, focus on anything other than Alex, the car accident, and the past year of my life. When I'm concentrating on not drowning, I can't think about any of that.

After my last lap, I exit the pool, grab the heated towel and the coffee the housekeeper set out for me, and wonder when, if ever, I will no longer need this distraction. It's been a year now, and I can't imagine the grief ever really leaving. I moved to London two weeks after Alex died, and it's become something of a ritual to drink my coffee while looking out at the garden. Alex hated it here, said it was "too cold and too old" for his liking, so we only ever came on business. I don't have many memories of the two of us here, which is perfect.

Even as I've watched the seasons pass through these windows—the roses bloom and wilt, the sky go from gray to grayer—I still wouldn't call the house I'm staying at home. For starters, it's a rental, completely modern and devoid of character, but there are only so many places with an eighty-degree indoor pool. It's been a safe place to land for the time being. But nothing about it is mine.

While here, I fear I've aged decades in a year and, at forty-one, have become a parody of a grieving widow. I'm suddenly a recluse who fills her days backstroking, knitting, and watching bad TV just to pass the time. I know I should feel grateful that I even have the option to withdraw from the world. And I am. It's one of the few privileges I've been more than happy to take advantage of. What else is money for, if you can't put an ocean between you and your past?

The modernist lounger I'm sitting on isn't something I would have ever chosen, and that psychological distance has been a comfort. In the days after the accident, I just couldn't handle the constant reminders of him around our house in Palo Alto—the spot on the counter where his electric toothbrush used to charge, the ancient couch in our screening room where we watched so many movies that there was a permanent dent in the cushion. And then there was his office: The one room that was solely his and the one place I didn't have decorating jurisdiction. He hadn't worked in it in years, but his piles of papers he'd never look at again, his favorite pens from Japan, the model airplanes he'd been making since childhood whenever he needed to slow down his thoughts—it's all still there, frozen in time. Afterward, I couldn't bring myself to even walk by that room, let alone go inside. And I didn't want anyone else to either, despite the staff's gentle offers. It was easier just to leave. To let someone pack me a few bags, schedule the plane, find a house.

Unfortunately, I figured out within a few weeks that time away from home would be more of a salve than a cure—not exactly a solution to my problems. Robyn said not to make any more major life changes in the first year, but there's an idea that's been nagging at me in the back of my mind for six months, and Robyn has only herself to blame. We were at the end of a particularly grueling session, and she asked me a question that I didn't know how to answer: "What would make you happy?" All I could think was that I knew what didn't: the $2.1 billion associated with Alex's name.

The word "billionaire" was used in the first line of every obituary for him, as if his forty-one years on Earth were only about the pursuit of money. I'm not naive enough to think that those things don't matter; I am a Black woman who grew up in America. But it was hard to see the person I love—loved—reduced to a single word that makes the world think they knew who he was, what he cared about.

It's not that Alex wasn't proud of the success that kind of money signified. He'd spent years grinding to get OneK off the ground, and selling the app to Facebook made it clear: His hard work paid off. Once the sale went through, our lives leapt from comfortably middle class to fuck-you money overnight. I went from Ndidi Davis, an unemployed woman having an identity crisis, to Ndidi Davis, the wife of one of the world's youngest billionaires having a (new) identity crisis. It was surreal. Head-spinning. It still is, eleven years later.

I take one final look out the window and pad back to the bathroom for my last shower. Today marks a year since Alex died, and it's my last day in London. Once I go home, I'm giving away 99 percent of our money—the money I feel no ownership over—to charity. I'm going to start over, and I'm going to do it on my terms. I just have to figure out what exactly those terms are.

1

Three Months Later, Palo Alto, California

I can count on my hands the number of times I've been able to do my laps before getting started on my never-ending to-do list for the foundation, but today is one of those rare mornings. The pain of missing Alex still hits me at peculiar times—I found an old sock under the bed last week, and it took twenty-four hours to recover—but staying busy helps.

After the pool and a shower, I pull on an old pair of Levi's and a poplin shirt, then meet Wendy, my chief of staff, in the dining room. Wendy's already seated at the table with the breakfast Chef Aaron made us in front of her.

"Good morning, Ms. Davis." Wendy turns off the screen of her iPad when she sees me walk in. With her perfectly blown-out salt-and-pepper bob, her tailored navy suit, and the warm gold eye makeup that complements her tan skin, she's the picture of elegant efficiency.

"Good morning, Wendy. Ndidi." I press a hand to my sternum as if I'm introducing myself.

Wendy just shakes her head; it's become a running joke between us that she's so formal with me and refuses to call me by my first name. At fifty-six, Wendy is used to working with high-profile politicians and is very much set in her ways. Our day-to-day was never as complicated as that of someone on Capitol Hill, so working for Alex and me for the past few years was an adjustment. I'm grateful she's stood by me through all of this, and I'm hoping that making her the coexecutive director at Giga means she'll stick around for the long haul. I can't handle the idea of starting over with someone else.

I take the seat next to her and start cutting my special protein pancakes like a grid. I don't remember the last time I cooked a meal for myself, and I can honestly say I don't miss it.

Wendy lets me eat a few bites before sliding a folder my way. Without looking, I know what it is.

She knows I know and eyes me expectantly. "We need to make a decision on this today."

"I don't want to," I tell her. The thought of talking to the press gives me anxiety.

"I know, and it's my job to make you. This kind of initial coverage will ensure the right people know about the work you're doing. You did say this was important to you."

I sigh. "You're right." I push my plate of half-eaten breakfast aside to look over the options again: a sit-down with Lesley Stahl at *60 Minutes*, a fluff piece for *People*, a chat on Meghan Sussex's podcast, or a profile in *Scale* by Geoffrey Campbell. "Stahl is probably our best option, but I don't think my nerves can take a TV interview," I manage.

Wendy nods. "Fair enough."

"I don't think *People* or Meghan's podcast are right. I can't handle touchy-feely real talk right now." The thought of keeping it together with Meghan's big brown eyes boring into my soul? Absolutely not.

"So, Geoffrey Campbell it is," Wendy decrees, then looks to me to affirm it. Instead, I shove a piece of now-cold pancake into my mouth.

"He scares you," Wendy says, reading me.

"They all do."

Which is true but not the whole truth.

I've never had the desire to talk to the media. Doesn't matter if it's something as innocuous as getting an A on a test or as jarring as my appendix bursting, my first impulse is to keep things to myself. Alex used to joke that in another life, I was a world-class spy, protecting state secrets at all costs. In any case, in this life, I am an overthinker with a strong desire to stay out of the spotlight. An overthinker who will override her instincts for the good of the foundation this one time.

Wendy sits a bit straighter somehow and rests her hands in her lap. "For what it's worth, I think he's the right choice. *Scale* has a global reach, and the fact that he knew Alex is a strength. He already has the background, so he can focus less on the past and more on what you're trying to do."

I nod along because everything she's saying is the best-case scenario. Geoffrey Campbell wrote the first, and arguably the best, profile of Alex when he was first starting OneK. He was there right as the app grew from a million users to thirty million, when celebrities like Snoop Dogg and the guys from Mischief were starting to use it. Reading Geoffrey's profile felt like getting to know the real Alex. He managed to capture Alex's idealism and tenacity, and also just how damn smart he was, in a way that made the public feel like he was a guy they could grab a beer with instead of one of the antisocial boy-genius types they'd come to expect. I don't need Geoffrey's writing to launch my own public persona, but I do want to be clear about my intention: In a world where wealth hoarding is not only possible but encouraged, I want to do the opposite. I want to give it all away, and I want to be clear and upfront about how I'll do it.

"He's a hell of a writer," Wendy offers. "Plus, there's a nice symmetry to it, for him to profile each of you. He's also willing to make certain concessions," she says, dangling the idea like a carrot on a stick. "He says he'll let us see the piece before it's published. He's already gotten the OK from his editors."

My eyebrows raise in surprise. "He's giving us editorial approval?"

"Well, I wouldn't go that far. He says he reserves the right to publish what he wants, but he's willing to give us a heads-up. Far from standard."

I can't argue. "Geoffrey Campbell it is."

"Great, I'll contact him this afternoon. You haven't met him, right?"

"No, my father had just had his heart attack, so I gave him a few quotes over email, but that's it."

Alex said Geoffrey was sharp and fair. That he had a

trick of seeming just unassuming enough to set his subject at ease and then throwing them a curveball when they least expected it. In the years since, I've read a few of his profiles—the president of Ukraine, the scammer who defrauded millions from the elderly in a Ponzi scheme—and he's only gotten better. His celebrity has also risen since he wrote a *New York Times* bestselling biography on Cooper Grant, an innovator in the tech for electric cars. I can't believe he's even interested in interviewing me, but I try not to question it. Too much.

11

A week later, Wendy's made good on her word and scheduled a sit-down with Geoffrey Campbell. I thought we'd do it over Zoom, but Geoffrey was adamant we do it in person.

I'm nervous. My anxious toe tapping is back. So is biting the inside of my lip. I've met presidents, foreign dignitaries, *Beyoncé*. But this is the first thing to matter to me in a deeply personal way in a long time, and I feel it.

Before I left this morning, Wendy reassured me again that the feature is the best way to satisfy the public's curiosity—about Alex's last days, his vision for the future, whether the Giving Pledge is something he would have actually gotten around to doing in his lifetime.

But as I sit waiting for Geoffrey, these talking points rattle around in my head less like a mantra and more like facts I have to remember for a big test.

"Would you like another drink?" A young Black woman wearing a server's crisp white Oxford shirt looks down at me expectantly. Like she's asked me more than once.

"Sorry, no. I'll stick with water for the time being. Thank you." I give her a wide smile, hoping I seem more at ease than I feel. She nods, topping off my glass before moving to her next table. I glance around and see the other lunch meetings in progress: A guy who looks like a young tech bro trying to reassure an investor about an upcoming IPO. An older couple bickering with each other, probably over splitting a Cobb salad and steak or getting their own. It's something Alex and I used to do, and I look away quickly before my heart can snag on it. My eyes land on an A-list author furiously typing on his computer. Probably his next critically acclaimed novel about an antihero white man with an underdeveloped wife.

Maybe The Battery wasn't the best meeting spot. I've never loved places like this that exist solely to shelter the rich and famous from the general public. It doesn't help that the only other person of color here is the waitress.

I pull out my knitting, an intricate cable pattern. What started as another Robyn-prescribed coping mechanism has become one of my favorite ways to pass the time.

"Ms. Davis?" At the sound of my name, I look up to find Geoffrey Campbell walking toward me. I know what he looks like from his media appearances, but in person, it's another story. He's . . . attractive. It's the first time that word has popped up in my mind about a man since Alex has been gone. Or the first time I've thought about it *and* my heart's started racing. His wavy black hair. His wide mouth. How he stands tall without seeming stiff. The fit of his clothes and the way they skim his body, hinting at what's underneath.

"I think you're the first subject I've ever had who beat me to the meeting spot." His easy smile creeps up to his deep green eyes, and my gaze catches on his thick lashes, the kind that, on men, seem deeply unfair.

I blush and feel grateful it doesn't show as much on my umber complexion. At least I hope it doesn't. "I'm not that early, am I?"

"Considering it's fifteen minutes until our one o'clock reservation and . . ." He points to my yarn and chuckles. The sound is full and just a little too loud, one of those contagious laughs that make me want to join in. But I just smile.

"My parents ingrained promptness in me." I shrug. "That and writing thank-yous."

"Good traits. Thanks for meeting with me." He sticks out his hand to shake, and I take it, surprised at how warm it is. Mine are always cold, a side effect of being anemic, but that doesn't explain the tingle I feel from the contact. It lingers as I brush my palm down my thighs, hoping the smooth wool of my trousers will mute the sensation.

Geoffrey slides into the seat across from me, fanning his napkin across his lap. "I know you had plenty of other options for this profile."

"I did. But no one else has our shared sense of . . . history." The acknowledgment feels fraught, but I've learned it's best to contend with the discomfort of Alex's death immediately so it doesn't loom.

"Ms. Davis—"

I hold up a hand to stop him. "Call me Ndidi. If we're going to be spending time together, you have to call me by my first name."

"Noted." He starts again. "Ndidi, you have my deepest

condolences. Alex was one of the most dynamic, compelling men I've ever had the pleasure of writing about."

"Thank you." I try to give my words weight without inviting more reflection. The past year has been an endless series of well wishes, sympathies, and prayers from loved ones and strangers, and at this point, their expressions of comfort feel almost perfunctory—sometimes painful. Something about the way Geoffrey's brow furrows, though, and the slight shake in his voice make me feel like there's something genuine there.

It feels personal, when I want to keep my distance.

I straighten the silverware in front of me and take a sip of water to clear my throat. "So, how will this work? I've never done this before." I've had media training and discussed this ad nauseam with Wendy, but I want to hear from him too.

Geoffrey leans forward in his chair as if he's letting me in on a secret. "We'll spend your kickoff week together. Mostly I'll follow you around for background, see your home, meet your chief of staff, that kind of thing." He pauses, his eyes scanning the room. "Did you bring any of your team here today?"

I shake my head. "Just me."

"That's interesting." His lips quirk with the hint of a smile.

"Why?"

He shrugs. "A lot of my subjects these days travel with their entourage—even if they linger in the background, someone is always there."

"The word 'entourage' gives me hives," I say without thinking. "I'm mostly with Wendy. And Bill, my driver, but they're pretty much the only team I had before all this. I don't plan on changing that."

I watch him watching me, perhaps trying to square what he knows about me from then with what he's learning about me now, like I'm doing with him.

"After next week, I'll come to the major events: the opening of the foundation—"

I interrupt him. "We're not having one of those. Too much pomp and circumstance." A lot of nonprofits get into trouble with bloated overhead, and while I doubt that will ever be the case with us, I don't want to get in the habit of excess spending.

"Right. In that case, I'll accompany you at any of the bigger meetings surrounding your donations."

I frown. I know I agreed to all of this, but reality is sinking in. He must be able to sense my trepidation. His eyes jump across my features. "The level of access you're giving me is very generous. It'll pay off, I promise."

"I believe that. It's just a lot."

"Can I ask, why did you agree to all this?"

I shrug. "It's what Alex's old publicist and Wendy both suggested. What they want."

"And what is it you want then?"

"If it were up to me, I'd be a private citizen." The words tumble out as if I can't help but be honest with him. "But Alex is, was, a public figure, and people are interested in his legacy."

"His legacy?"

My brow furrows with confusion. Did I say something wrong?

He rests his elbows on the table. "His legacy, not your own?"

"Yes, Alex's."

"Unless I'm mistaken, this is your idea. You're not continuing on a project Alex set up while he was alive, are you?"

I weigh my words. "No, it's not something we came up with together. I think Alex would have come to the idea in his own time, but he hadn't had a chance to get there yet." Alex had countless aspirations swirling around in his brain, and while this was never something we talked about explicitly, I believe it to be true. He was generous without grandstanding; he once gave five of his closest friends a million dollars each for no reason.

Geoffrey waits for me to continue but I don't. He nods with understanding. "I empathize with your desire for privacy, but I think people are interested in you too."

I laugh. Typically, anyone who tells me this is trying to get me to cut them a check. "I think the piece should focus on the foundation, not me."

Geoffrey leans back, and I see the wheels turning in his mind. "I think it can be about both. The foundation and the person behind it."

I shake my head. "No. My wealth is the only reason I'm of interest to people. I think, as a culture, we tend to believe people of means are better than they actually are."

He leans forward again. "Can you elaborate?"

It takes me a second to process that somehow this has turned from a casual conversation into one where I feel like I'm in the hot seat. "I thought this was just a preliminary meeting? We're off the record, right?"

"Yes, on both counts. You don't have to answer anything you don't want to. I'd just like to know what you think." His expression is open and curious in a way that doesn't feel performative—not like a journalist turning on his "active listening" face. I'm having trouble determining where Geoffrey Campbell the journalist and Geoffrey Campbell the man diverge.

"We make them more glamorous, more interesting than they are—it helps it make sense to people. I think the causes I'll help, the organization I'm setting up, and the people doing the day-to-day work are what's worth paying attention to."

"There's a lot of truth in what you're saying, but I think there's also an argument to make that wealth does allow people to be more interesting. I've interviewed my fair share of the ultrawealthy, and there's a common thread: They get to do or say whatever they want, with little to no consequences. I think the average person finds that compelling."

His words give me pause, and I sit back in my chair as I let my thoughts coalesce. "Sure, I think the choices people make are interesting, but that doesn't necessarily transfer to someone's personality or their values, things that actually make us who we are."

"Aren't we just a collection of the choices we make?"

His eyes gleam, and I can tell he gets a little kick out of debate. I hate to admit that it sparks something in me too.

"How we use our free will is fascinating. But I don't think watching people gild their own cages or do what they want for the hell of it—maybe it makes them assholes, but it doesn't make them *interesting*."

Geoffrey laughs, and for some reason, it feels like I won something.

I brush my hands against my pant legs again. "I just don't think the fact that I'm giving my money away makes me special."

"I guess you'll have to convince me." When he says this, there's a charge between us that wasn't there before. I feel it all around me—palpable, almost thick.

I reach for my glass only to find it's empty. My eyes race around the room for the waitress with an urgency that borders on desperation. I remind myself to breathe.

"Listen," he says, "this is my job. I think everybody has something about them that's worthy of a story. It's not always apparent at first glance, but that's where I come in. Leave that part up to me."

"So you're saying I should trust you?" My voice rises an octave, and I fear I sound like a schoolgirl.

"Exactly." His gaze drops, as if he's remembering where he is and just noticing the menu. He clears his throat. "Do you have any more questions for me?"

I have the sudden urge to ask something personal, but I don't let myself. "You mentioned following me for a week—is that Monday to Friday or all seven days?"

Geoffrey barks out a laugh. I frown, wondering if I worded the question the wrong way.

"It sounds like you're asking when I'll get out of your hair." I blush for the second time. I'm not used to being put on my back foot. It feels good. "I'd wager I'll be working on this story for the next two months or so. To be clear, I'll interview you first, a series of interviews over the next two weeks, and then I'll move on to the foundation's staff. I'll speak with some friends, family, and old coworkers, depending on what I need for background."

"That sounds very thorough." And like he'll be delving into OneK's origins, a topic I want firmly in the past, where I'd like to keep all my regrets. I'd thought about declaring OneK an off-limits topic as a condition of the profile, but I know Geoffrey doesn't work that way.

"Don't worry, you'll forget I'm there most of the time. Two months and I'm gone."

I try to keep a neutral face. "Two months is a long time. Where are you based?"

"Chicago." He studies me for a moment. "You seem surprised."

I try to tug my brows down. "No, it just seems like a lot of travel. A long time to be away from home."

He shrugs. "You get used to it."

I look down at his ring finger. It's bare. He catches where my gaze went, takes a sip of water, and clears his throat. "I'm single. Just me." Definitive, no room for misinterpretation.

I'm suddenly keenly aware that I'm still wearing my wedding band. Unsure how to respond, I open my phone as if to reply to a message but instead check my calendar to confirm what I already know: My week is filled with block after block of yellow, the times when Geoffrey's on my schedule. My heart bounces around in my ribcage.

This is going to be a long two months.

III

All afternoon, I find my thoughts circling back to Geoffrey. Wendy and I go over office logistics, but by the end of the workday, I'm still wired. As soon as I'm home, I plop down on the couch and call Adamma, who's three hours ahead in Richmond.

She picks up on the third ring. "Y'know, I was about to have sex with my husband."

"No, you weren't. For one, you barely put Jalen to bed. If anything, the two of you are about to watch whatever HBO show came on last night. Hi, Tyrique." It's Monday, and their schedule is like clockwork.

I hear Tyrique laugh in the background.

"One of these days, you're going to kill our mood."

"Don't pick up the phone then!"

Her tone softens. "I'll always pick up the phone."

"I'll do the same for you."

She's my baby sister and best friend. The second title is one she's grown into over the last five years, since she gave birth to Jalen. Something about seeing Adamma blossom into a mother has brought us closer and smoothed the edges where our personalities used to rub. Though she can still annoy me like no one else can.

"What's going on now?" She's doing something in the background. Putting away dishes, maybe.

"Nothing. Just wanted to call my favorite sister."

"Didi, I know you. Something is up. I can hear it in the way you're breathing."

"No, you can't." I take a deep breath just to be sure.

She chuckles, happy to get a rise out of me. "You had that meeting today with the journalist. How'd it go?"

"It was a bit . . ." I search for the word, not sure how much I want to admit. "Unexpected."

"In what way?"

"He's disarming for one. Really, uh, inquisitive."

"All things a journalist should be."

"Don't be a smartass. I guess I was just expecting someone more buttoned-up? The conversation had me a bit off balance the whole time. He's intense, but there's something almost playful about him too."

Adamma laughs. "Playful? It sounds like you think he's fine."

"I didn't say that!"

"Of course you didn't, but I'm just saying the quiet part out loud. How did you feel about that?" Adamma barrels on, knowing she's read the situation correctly.

"Don't put your therapist voice on."

"Number one, my voice is my voice. And number two, you're the one who called me—"

"And I'm beginning to wonder why I did." I sigh. Adamma's the person I process everything with. I just tend to forget how much I hate it.

"Girl, answer the question."

Now it's my turn to pause. I cross and uncross my legs on the couch, struggling to find a comfortable position. "I feel ridiculous. How am I noticing this guy's looks when I should be more concerned with what he's going to write about me?"

"Two things can be true at once: He's attractive, but he's also there to do a job."

"You make it sound so reasonable," I grumble back at her.

"Because it is! You're human, you have eyes. But it's not just about his looks; there's something else going on. You're like a duck: You appear calm on top, but I know you're kicking those little feet like mad underneath."

I'd rather be compared to a more elegant animal, like a cheetah perhaps, but the point stands. I sift through my thoughts. "I guess I'm scared. Public scrutiny is the last thing I want, but I do think it's the best way to avoid press in the future."

I never gave a public statement after Alex died, and by going into hiding, I'd inadvertently created even more mystery and speculation. Although I haven't been a public figure, Alex was. People looked up to him and wanted to know what he thought, so I feel like I do owe some sense of closure. Give them something now so I can get on with the rest of my life.

"Well, then shouldn't that bring you comfort? You're getting a chance to spotlight organizations you care about. Put that money to good use instead of hoarding it like most of those assholes do." Adamma has always pushed my thinking further to the left. She's the one who opened my eyes to the fact that in an ethical, just society, no one would be a billionaire. And still, the rich get richer. The notable exceptions like Chuck Feeney and MacKenzie Scott are giving away their money as fast as they can, responsibly—they're the people I look to.

"That's true . . ." I trail off, unsure how to articulate my thoughts.

"But?"

"But does it feel like I'm making Alex's death about me? He's only been gone a year, and I don't want it to feel like I'm trying to hijack his legacy."

"Listen, some people will think that. But they're the same Silicon Valley assholes who think all kinds of fucked-up things. You were an integral part of everything Alex did."

My mind wanders. Adamma doesn't know how integral to OneK's success I really was. Only three of us ever did, and one of us is dead, and another is off the grid.

Adamma keeps talking. "You were together your whole adult life and married for fourteen years. That money is your money. You're not doing anything wrong."

It's funny how I can intellectually know something, but if I don't feel it in my gut, then it doesn't make a difference.

"I'm not sure that you believe it yet," she continues,

building steam. "But I hope one day you will." We've had this conversation before, and I hear the sadness and slight impatience in her voice. I'd be sick of me too. We move on from my insecurities, and she gives me an update on Jalen's first week of kindergarten. After half an hour, I let her go. I know Tyrique is waiting for her to watch their show.

I think back to her words as I do my skincare, a routine that's only become more elaborate as I've gotten older and now includes one of those red-light masks. Alex used to make fun of me for wearing it, called me "Rose Gold Power Ranger" and asked when I was going to kick Rita Repulsa's ass. The first time he said it, I kicked him behind the knees instead.

While I try to prevent my own wrinkles, I wonder what Alex would have looked like with more of them. He was one of those guys who was getting better looking with age, as he grew into his gangly limbs and finally found the haircut that suited his wide-set brown eyes.

I find myself layering more creams and oils onto my dark-brown skin than makes sense for any one person, and I dawdle as I wrap my knotless braids up with a scarf. I dread climbing into bed. Sleeping alone hasn't come easy. I still miss having a human furnace next to me. I wrap the blankets around me, knowing I'll be cold no matter what.

IV

The next morning, Bill, my driver, drops me off at our new office in the heart of downtown San Francisco. I could have retrofitted one of Alex's old spaces into our headquarters, but I wanted the foundation to be a fresh start. The building is one of those skyscrapers that seem like they're at the center of the universe, filled with important people doing impressive things. Or at least that's what I thought when I was a kid. I arrive before everyone else except Wendy, who greets me with an iced coffee as soon as I open the door. I take a sip and groan. Pure pleasure. It's from Philz, the one franchise I missed while living abroad. The coffee is overly sweet and creamy, just the way I like it. "I've had about thirty of these since I've been back, but each one still hits like the first time."

Wendy laughs at my over-the-top reaction. "I don't know how you can stomach that stuff, but drink up. I want to give you the tour before anyone else gets in."

We secured this location a month ago, but this is my first time seeing it since our interior designer did her install. There are ten offices, a collection of cubicles, a conference room, and a kitchen. We've tried to warm up the standard setup with our color scheme of Sap Green, Dayroom Yellow, and Cardamom from Farrow & Ball alongside plush seating and quiet nooks to work from. I'd wanted our headquarters to look like the opposite of most tech spaces I've been in, with either stark white walls and zero thought to decor or exposed brick and ducts—some tired, hipster-kid idea of cool. The last room Wendy shows me is my corner office, only slightly bigger than the others but with a view facing the Golden Gate Bridge. There's a green couch across from the desk, and I can imagine myself squeezing in a nap or two on it. I'm quiet as I take it all in.

"So, what do you think?"

I know her well enough to know she's nervous, and I smile to assure her. "I love it. This is exactly how I imagined it."

"Not many people would do what you're about to do."

"What we're about to do."

Wendy shakes her head. "It's not my money." She waves a hand in the air. "This is all you."

I'm about to refute her claims again when there's a knock on the door. "Come in." I'm expecting to see Elijah Thomas, our program director, but it's Geoffrey Campbell. "Oh, hi. Welcome. Nice to see you again."

It's been a week since our meeting, and I'd been hoping he wouldn't be as good-looking as I remembered. But here he is, wearing a blazer and fitted jeans with a brown leather messenger bag slung over his shoulder, the picture of an intrepid reporter. His cheeks are flushed, his hair is slightly windblown, and I have the urge to fix a stray lock. I shake my head as if to dislodge the thought.

He steps into the office, gives Wendy a small nod in greeting. "I know I'm a bit early, but I wanted to get the lay of the land before the rest of your team got here. Hope I'm not interrupting anything."

Wendy takes a step forward. "You're not. We're about to run over Ndidi's speech."

"Are you OK with me watching you practice?" He turns toward me like he needs my explicit permission.

Even though I know he'll hear it later, the thought of that sends my heart rate into zone 3. "I'd prefer you didn't."

He looks disappointed but nods. "Understood."

As we stand in an awkward silence, I wonder if I was too harsh. But Geoffrey lifts up a finger, pointing to the cup sweating in my hand. "I find that place so overwhelming." His tone is playful, and the abrupt change makes me wonder if he's trying to put me at ease, a small kindness. He seems like a kind man. I push the thought aside when I realize he's waiting for a response.

"You know that's sacrilegious to say around here. Takes some trial and error to find your blend, but I'm a Philtered Soul person myself. Equal ratio sugar to caffeine is the secret."

"That sounds disgusting." But he's grinning, and I am too. Nothing I said was funny, but for whatever reason, I feel giddy. Which is not a feeling I'm used to.

Wendy clears her throat, a reminder that she's still in

the room with us. We both turn our attention to her. She raises her eyebrow in a way that tells me she noticed our rapport, but I shake my head back at her, indicating there's nothing to see here.

"Geoffrey, why don't I show you where you can set up? And Ms. Davis, why don't you go over today's agenda before we start?" It's more of a command than a question. And she's right. At this stage in the game, I can't get distracted by a man I barely know.

I sneak a look into the boardroom and scan the faces of nine full-time staffers and the seven board members, all of whom Wendy and I selected with painstaking care.

I'm about to go in when Elijah walks up and gives me a hug. "Nice to see you, boss lady."

"Good to see you too." I smile back at him. Elijah is the get I'm the most excited about. A queer Black man who got his degree in nonprofit management from Harvard, Elijah has worked everywhere from grassroots organizations to upper management at some of the biggest national players. It took a lot of convincing to get him to join a limited-life foundation, especially since career longevity is antithetical to the work. But Wendy and I were able to persuade him that he'd be able to do more good, more effectively, more quickly than anywhere else. Give us ten years, we argued, and then you can go anywhere. Once we got him, the rest of the staff followed.

Elijah opens the door for me, and I take a seat next to Wendy and nod hello to the room. I know everyone here on some level, but it's still nerve-wracking to be the center of attention. I've hated public speaking since the sixth grade, when I was supposed to recite a portion of Martin Luther King Jr.'s "I Have a Dream" speech and promptly threw up when it was my turn. Took me the rest of middle school to live that one down. I think about what Adamma always says—that the key is to believe that everyone in the room wants you to do a good job, which I know is true. There's a slight shake in my hand as I take a sip of water from the glass set before me. I stand up. I make eye contact with Geoffrey, who's set up in the corner, a fly on the wall. When I asked Wendy if it was strange to include him in our very first meeting, she assured me the work we want to do isn't top-secret intel and that she could always ask him to leave. He gives me a small smile, and it feels like something private, just between us.

I thank everyone and tell them how proud I am to be starting this undertaking with them. And then I pause, not expecting to feel so emotional. I take a deep breath. "There are so many critical problems facing the world, and it's imperative to me that we're intentional about how we allocate the money over the next decade," I begin again. "We will start with five core areas of focus: early childhood education, women's health care and abortion access, the homeless crisis in California, gender equality in Nigeria, and global health."

Just saying these words aloud makes the initiative feel more real. I move on to logistics—shorter-term versus longer-term goals, the scale of the organizations we'll partner with. "I want to make sure this is collaborative. I've been in environments where that wasn't the case, and that's not a dynamic I want to re-create here," I say in closing.

I look around the room, connecting with each person at the table. It's an important part of my message, and I want to make sure the point lands.

Everyone claps when I'm done, and I soak it in. As much as I was dreading the moment, I know I'm in a safe space. I sit down, and Wendy opens the floor for remarks.

Henry Jacobson, one of the board members, is the first to speak up. Henry is one of those white guys who looks straight out of central casting for "businessman"—tall with graying hair, a porcelain smile, and a lifelong membership to the boys' club.

Alex met Henry at a start-up conference during the early days of OneK and came to see him as a bit of a mentor, since he was ten years older and had already made a few million by his early thirties. They never worked together but were thinking of collaborating on something just before Alex died. Henry's a bit too much of a frat guy for my taste, but I do believe he has strong instincts when it comes to tech investment that I hope are translatable.

"Ndidi, thank you so much for your eloquent remarks." Interesting adjective choice but I choose to ignore it. "While I think those are all areas of importance, I don't see anything about tech or STEM programs on that list."

"You're right. That's not currently a priority. I thought long and hard, and this is where I landed." The last part comes out a bit softer than what I wanted. Henry opens his mouth again but catches himself—instead, he just purses his lips and nods. Out of the corner of my eye, I see Wendy shoot me a nod of reassurance. "Any other questions?"

The rest of the meeting is fruitful, but it's not lost on me that Henry is quiet, almost sullen. He speaks up again right before we adjourn. "I think we've made some great progress here today, but I don't want Alex to get lost in all this. Have you considered naming the foundation after him?"

I see Geoffrey scribble something in his notebook.

"That's a valid question," I say. "But I wanted something a bit more anonymous. Alex and I aren't the kind to want our names on buildings."

Henry looks over at Geoffrey. "Anonymous! I guess that's why he's here then."

I freeze. Everyone laughs. I know I'll look like a spoilsport if I don't join in.

"Good one," I say, fighting to keep a smile on my face. "It won't be a habit to talk to the press, but I thought it would be a good way to get our message out there. Allow organizations to find us."

"I'm just teasing, Didi. I think the press is good." He gives Geoffrey a thumbs-up. Geoffrey's eyes bounce back over to me, a slight frown on his face. He's bent forward in his chair with his elbows on his knees, almost like he would pounce if he could.

"For what it's worth," another board member, Nicole Edwards, chimes in, "I like Giga Giving as a name. I feel like it's a subtle nod to OneK, and it outlines what we're doing here." She's the creator of one of the first mobile dating apps, and I can tell by the knowing smile she flashes me that she's had to deal with plenty of men like Henry.

As everyone files out of the room, I stand by the door to shake their hands and thank them for coming, and Henry is the last board member to leave. "Didi," he says, overly familiar as usual. *That nickname is reserved for my friends, my loved ones,* I want to say. "I didn't mean to put you on the spot back there. I just think you need to get more of Alex in here. I mean, we wouldn't be here without him, right?"

"It's OK, the meeting was the correct venue to give your opinion." I don't think he's intending to remind me that my dead husband is the only reason I have this money in the first place, but it sure feels like it.

"Henry." I pause. "I think about Alex every day. I don't need any help on that front. I'll think about your STEM idea though." If there's a bite in my tone, I can't prevent it.

"That's all I ask. We're on the same team here." He pats me on the back like he's my Little League coach. After he finally leaves, I sink down in the chair closest to me and wonder if I'm in over my head. I hear a shuffle behind me and notice that Geoffrey's still in the room, packing up his messenger bag. I feel a pang of tenderness toward him.

"Was that the most incompetent board meeting you've witnessed?" I ask.

Geoffrey laughs. "Not even in the top ten. I was in the meeting when the CoLab founder fired everyone over Zoom."

"I feel like not calling everyone 'incompetent babies

who can't locate their own anuses' is a low bar, but I'll take it."

He laughs and walks closer to me. My body registers how near he is, and I shoot up out of my chair without thinking.

He stops in his tracks. "So, tell me, why'd you decide to have a board in the first place? You could technically just write checks as you please, right?"

"I could, but I like the idea of organizations pitching to a foundation rather than to me as a private citizen."

"I'm sure you get a lot of that."

I nod. "Enough to delete all my social media."

"Even your OneK profile?"

"Even my OneK." I chew on the rest of my answer. "More than that, I'm just one person. One person with a singular worldview and set of experiences. I want to start with what matters to me in my bones, but I think there's a danger in using money to shape the world based solely on what I think is right, so I need to have a team of people around me with their own perspectives."

He nods, considering. "Even when they don't always agree?" It's obvious he's referring to Henry.

"Even then."

"A 'team of rivals' approach to philanthropy?" He taps a finger on his lower lip, like he's testing out a theory.

"I wouldn't go that far. I don't want someone diametrically opposed to everything I believe in. I don't think anyone on the board is like that." In saying it, I'm wondering how much I can color his perception of today's meeting.

Geoffrey nods. He takes a step forward, and I take one back, knocking into the edge of the table. I cringe.

"I'm gonna get going," he says.

I try to flatten my expression. "Of course. Thank you for your time."

"Oh, you'll be getting plenty more of that." He gives me a small wave.

When he walks out the door, I press my palms to the table and splay my fingers. I remind myself to breathe.

The rest of our kickoff week proceeds at a breakneck speed. The whole board is in town, and we have stacks of research packages to sift through. It's embarrassing for me to admit even to myself, but this is only the second adult job I've had, and my body and my brain are not used to being in meetings all day. It's exhausting making so many decisions, but exhilarating too, to know that I'm actually doing something worthwhile.

In our final meeting of the week, there's an ongoing debate about how much money we should allot to Sic, a charity that provides health-care advocates to low-income people living with sickle cell anemia. I want to push for a more significant $4 million to start, but Henry thinks we should be more conservative out of the gate and only give a quarter of that.

"The point of what we're doing here is to make big, effective changes," I argue for the third time.

"But Sic has only been around for four years; they've barely had enough time to figure out their whole strategy," Henry pushes back. He sounds as frustrated as I feel, but I try to keep my tone measured for risk of sounding angry or being thought of as aggressive.

"Your point is not without merit, but that's where our money can make all the difference. So many of these on-the-ground programs fail because of a lack of investment, so—"

Henry barrels past me. "That's very well, but it doesn't mean we should ignore logic when we have another program that's well established that we could partner with."

I'm too stunned to process the fact that he spoke over me without a second thought to respond.

Wendy mouths, *OK?* and I nod despite feeling embarrassed. I don't want to make a thing out of it. I know having a thick skin is a part of this, but I'm starting to feel like every conversation with Henry requires jousting.

Elijah speaks up. "Look, Henry, you may be right about the tested viability of the national foundation, but there's a real opportunity here with Sic. The founder, Maya, is a young Black woman, and she has public interest right now because of all the work she's done on social media. So many of these patients don't have the time to sort through all the red tape to get good health care."

Elijah is sharp and convincing, and I feel the room coalesce around his point.

Wendy, ever the diplomat, steps in to formalize the agreement. "We'll set up clear goal posts in the grant contract as well as timelines and reporting dates for the release of each installment of funding. Sound good?" She makes it seem like she's speaking to all of us, but it's clear her statement is to placate Henry. He nods. I'm surprised he doesn't verbalize his point to have the last word.

After the meeting, Henry once again corners me on his way out of the door. "Things got a little heated back there. I'm just really passionate," he says with a shrug. I wait for an actual apology, but he gives me a sheepish grin, one I'm sure he perfected back in his college days and has been deploying on women ever since.

He taps his fingers on the doorframe. "I just want to make sure it's an environment where dissent is not only OK but actively encouraged. I know that's the kind of workplace Alex ran, and it's what I'm used to."

I put on my best poker face, my version of his sheepish grin. "Of course. But at the end of the day, we all have shared common goals, right?"

"Right. By the way, I sent you some programs to consider. Take a look." Henry walks out, leaving me feeling like I'm his employee instead of his boss.

V

I'm still reeling after the meeting. Henry's callout has gotten under my skin. I know I'm supposed to be trusting my instincts, but after a lifetime of second-guessing myself, it doesn't come easily to me. Henry and Alex subscribed to a "move fast and break things" mentality, which plays in the tech world with its "minimum viable products" and "iterate or die" ethos. But that's not what we're doing over here in the world of philanthropy—we're trying to fix what the world has already broken, an approach that requires a lighter touch.

I look over some of the options Henry sent, and it's a lot of what I expected, STEM program after STEM program. There's a knock on my door. "Come in."

It's Geoffrey, looking more trepidatious than usual, with his ever-present notepad, pen, and phone in hand. "I was waiting in the conference room, but it didn't seem like you were coming any time soon."

I steal a look at the clock and see that it's a little after seven. Our sit-down was scheduled for six. "Oh shit, I completely forgot. I'm sorry it—"

He holds up a hand to stop me.

"Don't apologize. You're not the first person who's forgotten a meeting."

"Doesn't make me feel like any less of an asshole." To already be drowning a week in doesn't bode well for me long term.

"You're hard on yourself." An observation, not a question.

"Alex used to tell me that all the time. As much as things change, they stay the same." I say the last part softly, more to myself than him. "Take a seat."

"You're still OK to do this? We can reschedule."

I grimace. "You've seen my schedule."

He laughs. "You're right." His gaze softens as he looks me over. "But really, I know it was a long day." He's kind enough not to mention Henry by name.

"I look that bad?" I haven't been sleeping well, and I'm sure the bags under my eyes have taken over my whole face, monthly facials be damned.

"I would never say you look bad. I'm not sure that's possible." He coughs, and I notice his cheeks have the slightest bit of color to them.

"I have a good dermatologist," I say, trying to downplay how flustered I'm feeling.

Geoffrey doesn't say anything, bites the inside of his cheek as if he's physically stopping himself from responding.

He sits. Finally. He places his phone on my desk and asks if it's OK to record. I give him my consent, but he doesn't immediately begin asking questions. Instead, he skims his notepad. His handwriting looks like chicken scratch—like boy handwriting—and I have no luck in trying to decipher any of it.

Geoffrey's mostly been a silent presence over the week, quietly taking notes while the rest of us talk, but he's becoming more and more familiar. He keeps his face neutral most of the time, but there are tiny microexpressions I'm starting to pick up on—the furrow in his brow when Henry interrupts, the slight lift of his right eyebrow when he's intrigued, or the way he tilts his head back when he's deep in thought. His mind seems to be constantly working, churning information over. It's fascinating to watch.

I know I should be able to ignore him, but I find my eyes drifting his way during meetings. There have been a few instances where we made eye contact through the glass windows in my office, and I had to pretend to yawn or look down to take notes. It's ridiculous, but I keep having flashbacks to my high school self, obsessing over Billy Preston in math class, a boy who had no idea I existed. It feels like misplaced energy, same as then.

"Why don't you tell me about your upbringing?" Geoffrey asks, snapping me out of my thought spiral.

"That feels like the start of a therapy session." I fold my arms across my chest.

"I promise not to psychoanalyze you." He does a scout's honor for good measure.

"OK. Well, I grew up in Virginia with my baby sister, Adamma, and our parents. They immigrated from Nigeria."

"What brought them to the U.S.?"

"Opportunity. A more stable government. They were both in high school during the civil war, so America was a better option for college. They came here with nothing, but eventually my dad ran an insurance agency, and my mom was a teacher."

"Was? She retire?"

"Yeah. My dad still has his agency, but they spend half the year in Nigeria now."

"What was it like growing up with immigrant parents?"

"A bit of a challenge. They were hard on us, pushed us to do math and science so we'd become a doctor or an engineer. A lawyer if we wanted to do something more creative."

He laughs, and a part of me thrills at that. "I forgot—a nurse is OK too. Though nurse practitioner is better. Anyway, I think I have the typical first-generation story." I notice his right eyebrow rise at this. "What?" I ask.

"'Typical' isn't a word I'd use to describe someone who became a billionaire by their late twenties."

"Well, it's the least I could do after not getting a master's degree."

Geoffrey laughs again, and it warms me. "How did the two of you meet?"

"Don't you already know this from Alex's profile?" It's a pretty run-of-the-mill story.

"In theory. But each person tells a story in a different way. So I'd like to hear it from you."

"OK. We were both in the same computer science course our freshman year. It took me a while to notice, but he'd go out of his way to sit next to me every class. Never said more than hi to me most days, but he arrived late one day and had to go ask three people to move down so he could get the seat next to me. That's when I realized, *Oh, this guy is into me.*"

I smile at the old memory. "Looking back, I realize he was nervous, but I didn't think I was someone he would think was intimidating."

Geoffrey shakes his head but doesn't say anything.

"Anyway, after class I told him that I'd save him a spot from now on if he wanted, and he said he'd like that. We ended up walking around campus for four hours that day, talking about nothing and everything. We were pretty inseparable after that."

"Bold move on his part. One of those moves that's creepy from the wrong person but endearing from the right one." We both laugh. Something in me lightens with this forced proximity to my younger self.

"It was. It could have backfired for sure, but I recognized something in him that he saw in me."

"What was that?"

"That we were both loners looking for the person who understood us. I think that was the real foundation of our relationship. We had this innate understanding of the other person's intentions. Even when we weren't on the same page, I always knew where he was coming from. You don't find that often." I look up to find Geoffrey staring at me with something in his eyes I can't read.

"No, you don't." He looks down to jot down a note, and

my eyes rest on his ridiculous lashes. "Alex got the idea for OneK in college, right?"

"He did." I launch into the story I've told for years now. "When we were seniors, my mom's family lost their home in Nigeria. A freak electrical storm caused a fire. They lost pretty much everything, but the thing they were most heartbroken about was the family photo albums. I was upset because there were so many photos I never had the chance to see, since we hadn't been to Nigeria in ten years. I never got to see pictures of my mom growing up."

"I'm sorry that was taken from you." His voice drops, tinged with the same warmth and concern as his condolences over Alex.

"I am too." I pause, and a gentle ripple of grief washes over me. "Smartphones were gaining popularity, and having pictures in our pockets was becoming the new normal. And Alex's mind went into problem-solving mode: 'What if there was an app that allowed everyone to share their memories as photos, in real time across borders?' Obviously, Facebook was starting to be a thing, but that was confined to college campuses, and it was so much about expressing yourself through your status, writing on walls. Alex thought images were a more effective way to communicate."

"A picture is worth a thousand words."

"Exactly, so OneK was born." I grin. "He originally wanted to call it The 1000th, but I thought the branding of OneK was cooler. Who knows."

"You helped him come up with the name?"

"I did. My one and only contribution." My heart speeds up at the lie, but I'm practiced enough at it that I know it doesn't show. After fifteen years, it's become second nature. I've hidden the truth from every single person in my life besides Alex: He came up with the idea but couldn't crack the codebase for the app. After weeks of trial and error, I figured it out. A long time ago, we decided to leave that part out of the story.

I smile at Geoffrey, expecting this to be where his line of OneK questioning ends. In the past, once it's been made clear I'm just the wife, people lose interest. But Geoffrey just looks at me, expectant.

"It was Alex's baby. I didn't want to mix business and our personal lives." I tap my pointer finger against the desk, a nervous habit. But I stop when Geoffrey's eyes follow my movements.

"I would think that since programming is what you studied, and the idea of the app came from something so personal to your family, you'd want a part in it. You graduated cum laude, one of the best in your class. Wouldn't it make sense for Alex to lean on your talents?"

"Look, not everyone wants to work with their partner. He didn't need me. Besides, he met Danny Oliveira early on." Danny was Alex's cofounder, a guy Alex met through mutual friends. Danny taught himself how to code as a kid, and he always had an interest in psychology. At Stanford, he studied symbolic systems, their term for what is basically cognitive science, a great basis for designing user-friendly software. Danny's a bit of an eccentric, an adrenaline junkie who left the tech world and an internet connection behind to chase waves after they cashed in.

Geoffrey shifts forward in his chair and taps his bottom lip. "I spoke to him when I wrote the Alex piece. Interesting guy. I do remember him speaking highly of you, in fact. I was rereading some of my transcripts to prep, let me see." Geoffrey flips through his notes. "He said you had a 'big brain.' You never helped them out with anything?"

"No," I snap. I'm officially over this line of questioning. Geoffrey's persistent in a way I'm not used to dealing with. I'm usually in a position to give the cookie-cutter answer or sit it out entirely.

"OK. Where did you end up going? I couldn't find employment records of you at any other company. Not even a start-up."

"That's because the one I joined barely lasted eight months."

Geoffrey waits for me to elaborate. I don't. This part of my life isn't something I relish talking about.

"What kind of work was it?"

"It was health care related. An app to streamline the medical billing process. But the guy behind it was a bit of a prick."

"In what way?"

"He pretty much covered the abusive-boss playbook: derogatory language, racism, sexism. He was probably homophobic too, but no one we worked with was openly queer."

"Did you make the choice to leave, or did the project fall apart?"

"I left. I was the only woman of color there, and I couldn't really handle it."

"It sounds like a toxic environment."

"It was. But it was also just *the* environment."

"What do you mean?"

"Every place was like that. Any time I went to a women-in-STEM mixer, I was inundated with nightmare stories. I thought maybe having an HR department would help, but turns out, that's not what HR departments are for: They're to protect the company. I said no to the next three job offers I got."

"What was your next move?"

I know Geoffrey is just doing his job, but I can't help but begrudge the curious glint in his eyes. I sigh, feeling like I'm back in the shoes of that scared, overwhelmed, twenty-three-year-old girl. "Alex's grandparents had given him some money to get OneK off the ground. It wasn't a million like people say—more like thirty thousand, which was still a third of their retirement savings. They took a gamble on him. But anyway, he had enough to split rent and basic necessities with two other guys while he developed the app. I moved in with him and bounced around temp jobs, trying to figure out what I wanted to do. It's not a time in my life I'm proud of. Playing housewife was not exactly a life goal. My parents were disappointed in me for giving up so easily."

"They didn't have compassion?"

"No. For them, the answer is always to put your head down and do the work. But I tried that, and it just made me feel angry. And then numb. Plus, I saw how invigorated Alex was by OneK, and I knew I'd never have that."

"So would you say you've made peace with quitting the tech industry?"

"Are you a therapist now?" I try to keep my tone light, but there's an edge I can't shake. "You sound like my sister." Before I can think too much about the way this man sees through me, my stomach rumbles loud enough for him to hear it. It breaks the tension in the room, and both of us laugh. "I skipped lunch today," I tell him. "Have you eaten?"

He shakes his head no.

"Why don't you come back to the house with me, and I can order something? We can talk while we eat." The suggestion slips out of me before I can overthink it.

Geoffrey looks caught off guard but recovers quickly, if only to save me from embarrassment. "Oh, sure. I'd love that." We agree to gather up our stuff and meet downstairs. As I flick off my lights and shut my office door, I'm desperate not to think about the fact that I just invited this man to my *home*, but I can't help but notice that I feel a lot less exhausted than I did twenty minutes ago.

VI

We're silent most of the drive. Riding home is usually my place to unwind, kick my heels off, and replay the day, but in Geoffrey's presence, I'm sitting up straight, feeling restless. There's enough space between us in the backseat that we're not in danger of touching, yet every cell in my body is aware of his movements. I realize I'm sweating and point the air vents toward my neck. He's not a manspreader, but he's relaxed, leaning his shoulder against the door.

It's not until we pull up to the gate that Geoffrey looks over at me and finally speaks. "You moved?"

I shake my head in confusion. "No, we've—I've lived here for the last five years." And then, I put it together. "You watched our old *Architectural Digest* video."

"Of course I did. Research."

I shake my head again, now in embarrassment at what else he might have consumed about me, and Geoffrey raises that right brow again. "Sometimes I forget how much of my life is already out there," I say.

"Is that something that bothers you?"

"You know how you can't get toothpaste back in the tube? It's kind of like that."

Bill pulls around the curved driveway, and I look out the window, hoping Geoffrey won't press me on my non-answer. Instead, he asks, "Why'd you sell the old place?"

"Alex always thought of it as a starter home. It was three times bigger than the house I grew up in. But when we found this place, I couldn't say no."

"But what about that garden? It seemed like there was a lot of work put into it." He sounds genuinely concerned. It's almost touching.

"Not personally," I say, amused. Sometimes I forget that most people have no idea how much staff is involved when there's a "B" attached to your net worth. "Why, do you garden?"

Geoffrey shakes his head. "No, but it's one of those hobbies I say I'll get into when I retire. I'm not home enough to keep a houseplant alive."

"Not even a succulent?"

"Even a succulent deserves care. It might be OK on its own for a while, but all living things thrive with a little love and attention."

It feels like he's talking about more than just botany. I find myself drawing closer to him, but then I remember who he is, and I lean away, look intently at something out of my window again. I clear my throat. "The garden here is even better," I manage. "You'll see."

I give Geoffrey a tour, and I can tell he genuinely likes it.

He marvels at the craftsmanship of the house, originally built in the 1950s. I order us Thai food and then leave him alone in the kitchen while I change. Despite this being an interview, I refuse to wear structured clothes in my own home. We set up camp in the living room, my favorite in the house because of the skylights and wooden beams on the ceiling. I take a seat on the floor—it's my default, where I feel most comfortable. Geoffrey sits down next to me, only a pillow's width away, and my back straightens with surprise. He looks right at home, like he's been here before and will be again.

I expect him to jump right into the same line of questioning from the office, but he throws me a curveball. "OK, why don't we play a game?"

"A game? That doesn't sound professional." Never mind that he's about to see me slurp pad Thai in drawstring cashmere pants.

"Yes, a game. For every question I ask you, you get to ask me one." We lock eyes, and it's almost like a taunt.

"Is this because I haven't been forthcoming? Are you trying to trick me into loosening up?"

Geoffrey shrugs. "You'd be surprised at how many politicians I've had to break this out for."

"I'm not sure that makes me feel better. But fine."

"Let's start there. How are you feeling?" A softball.

"Tired. A little agitated." Those truths are easy to admit. He nods, waits for me to ask him something. "OK. Why did you want to interview me?" I've been dying to know this since before we met.

He tilts his head back, and I know he's weighing his words. "At face value, this is a compelling human-interest piece. The intersection of tech, philanthropy, how the wealthy use or don't use their money for good. There's a tragedy, the death of a young CEO, and of course, the story of the beautiful widow he left behind."

My mind catches on the word "beautiful." I have to swallow it down. He taps his pen against his notepad. "But something always felt unresolved about this story."

"In what way?" I brace myself, wondering if he already knows the truth and is just waiting for the right opportunity.

"This story was so pivotal to my career. We're all the same age, but Alex was able to do something that changed the world in such a short amount of time. I know people downplay social media, but OneK created entire industries, connected people in unprecedented ways, documented all of life's moments, from birth announcements to war and revolution. I guess I always thought I'd have an opportunity to talk to him about how that weighed on him, years later."

I'm quiet, considering what I should say, and surprised at how sincere he's being. There's a tenderness to it that makes me want to be soft in return. But I also don't want to give myself away. "I think, if Alex were here, he would say it's the best feeling and the worst feeling. It's been a tool to unite the world just as much as it has been one to drive it apart—so much of social media has made us more insecure and disconnected. Combative with each other. It's gone way beyond the scope of what he originally set out to do, and because of that, the app doesn't really feel like his anymore." At least that's how I've had to rationalize my feelings about it.

Geoffrey nods and rolls up the cuffs of his shirt, a white Oxford that looks like it's been washed a hundred times. The fact that I'm distracted by his forearms only serves to underscore the attraction I denied to Adamma.

"Sorry," he starts again. "I didn't mean to get us side-tracked. I want to know more about you. Do you, or did you ever, think about going back to the tech world? To start something of your own?"

"Y'know, it's not exactly fun to talk about my career failures. I learned a long time ago that the only thing what-ifs do is keep you up at night."

"Huh. Well, this is the only thing I've done. Though, I've had my fair share of jobs go wrong. I was fired from the first two papers I worked for. I actually lucked into the interview with Alex after a buddy from J-school recommended me. I had a lot riding on that piece, and I was lucky it turned out so well."

"I didn't realize. So, what made you become a journalist in the first place?" I ask, noticing my own genuine curiosity. It's starting to feel like a regular conversation, not a tit for tat.

"It's the only thing I've wanted to do. When I was a kid, my mom used to drop me and my sister off at my grandma's house for the weekend so she could work extra waitressing shifts. She'd pick us up Monday morning and take us to school."

"You had a single mom?"

"For a time. My dad left her for another woman when I was five, eventually moved to South Carolina. We spent most summers with him. My mom met my stepdad when I was thirteen."

There's an edge to his tone that wasn't there before, and I sense there's something behind it. "You didn't get along with him?"

"No. It was a mix of me trying to be the man of the house and puffing up my chest at any change he wanted to make. He was one of those guys who thought being a good husband just meant bringing home a good paycheck. He wasn't really there emotionally."

I let him sit with it for a moment. "That must have been hard." It's a paltry statement, but I'm not sure how much more to pry.

He bites his cheek. "Anyway. My grandma had a ritual of sitting down to watch *60 Minutes* while we ate Sunday dinner. She was a surprisingly liberal white woman in rural North Carolina. She always told us that Andy Rooney and Dan Rather were the only men she trusted." He laughs at the memory, and I shift a few inches toward him, like that will bring me closer to the story. Like it'll help me see how he became the person he is now. I picture the two of them in front of the TV, surrounded by their gumption.

"But more importantly, she taught me to question the people in power, to never take no for an answer, and to do my own research—like, actual research, not the modern quick-internet-search kind. I feel like those are my life tenets as well as my journalistic ones."

"Sounds like your grandmother was a smart woman. Convicted."

"She was. She pushed me to sign up for the newspaper in middle school, and I never looked back."

"What were you like as a kid?" I know it's not my turn to ask a question, but it seems like we left the game by the wayside three rounds ago. I can't help it. Suddenly I want, need, to know.

Geoffrey runs a hand through his hair, and it looks windblown like it did that first day at the office. A quiet huff escapes from his lips. "Kind of a loser." He softens when he sees my expression and gives an exaggerated wince at his word choice.

"I think I had a bit of a chip on my shoulder and saw myself as an outcast, since most of the kids at school were either preps or rednecks, and I was neither. Even without my grandma's influence, writing makes sense for kids who feel like outcasts."

"A rebel with a cause." I reframe that last part to put a positive spin on it.

His eyes crinkle as he smiles at my corny joke, and he stretches his legs out in front of him. "What about you? How was little Ndidi growing up?"

"I didn't have too many friends growing up, so I was kind of a *loser* too." I put emphasis on the word.

"OK, yes, I hear how bad that sounds now. Thank you

for demonstrating. Consider it a banned word. Deal?" He holds out his hand for me to shake.

"Deal." I take his hand, and I'm brought back to the first time I met him, only a few weeks ago. How can it be only that long? If I felt butterflies at that lunch, then what I'm experiencing now is an earthquake, sudden and life altering. I pull my hand back, startled. I notice that somehow we've both moved an inch closer to each other. I press my palms against my thighs and turn back to my story. "I stuck out like a sore thumb in school. I was often the only Black kid in any of my classes, and the only with immigrant parents. I think I was called 'the Black girl' more than I was called my name." The memories grate, even now.

"That's horrible."

I like that he doesn't question if I'm serious or if I'm exaggerating. He takes me at face value, plain and simple. This isn't exactly standard from white people.

"It was. But it should have prepared me for college and the tech world. I was definitely the only Black woman in those rooms. Only woman most times." This time when I express the sentiment, it's less fraught than how I said it earlier. Somehow, without me realizing it, my guard is down.

"We don't have to keep talking about this if you don't want to. You've had a long day."

I read his expression, looking for signs that this is some kind of trick to lure me into greater ease. If he's deceiving me, though, there's not an obvious tell. He just looks at me like one human to another, an empathetic listener willing to hear my story.

"I'm OK." I pause, gather my thoughts. "Turns out, being wealthy kind of works the same way. I'd go to these parties, these galas, with Alex, and ninety percent of the crowd was just old white men with their much younger wives. Maybe if they were on the third or fourth one, they'd be with a woman of color. It was always shocking to them that Alex and I were the same age. One guy, a CEO of a Fortune 500 company, told him I was a good choice for a starter wife."

"What the fuck? He said that in front of you?"

It's the sharpest I've heard his voice, and it gives me a buzz. I shake my head. "I don't think he knew I was there. He was probably already four drinks in."

"That's not an excuse."

"I'm not saying it was, just a fact."

He's quiet for a moment. "And how did Alex respond?"

The question throws me. Do I tell or do I protect Alex? If I were talking to anyone else, I know I would sugarcoat it, but despite Geoffrey's job and the fact that he could use this against me, I trust him.

"He laughed."

"Ndidi—"

I interrupt before he can admonish me for defending him. "I don't think he realized I was there either. And when I brought it up to him later, when *I* was four drinks in and still pissed, he apologized. Groveled, really. He told me he responded that way out of shock."

"You don't need to make up an excuse for him." Geoffrey grips his knee, his knuckle whitening from exertion. Using himself like a stress ball to contain his anger, but it looks like it hurts.

I have an instinct to comfort him. Without thinking, I reach over and put my hand on top of his. I feel his hold loosen up as he relaxes at my touch.

It's a heady thing.

One second, two seconds, three I allow myself before pulling away. I stand up abruptly. "Do you want a glass of wine?" We haven't been drinking, and I know alcohol isn't the most professional element to add to the equation, but sometimes it's the only thing that'll do. If Geoffrey has any hesitation, he doesn't show it when he nods eagerly.

"Red or white?"

"Whatever you're drinking." Geoffrey moves to get up, but I gesture for him to stay seated. I need a moment alone to shake this feeling of attraction.

I grab a bottle I shipped back the last time I was in Bordeaux and dole out two heavy pours. Once my heart rate returns to normal, I carry back both glasses and the bottle with me. When I sit down, I'm mindful to put more distance between the two of us.

We both take our first sips; an awkward tension permeates the air. "This is good." Geoffrey offers.

"Thanks. We first had it at a state dinner in France. It's my favorite now."

Geoffrey laughs, and I smile, unsure of what's funny.

He must sense my confusion. “Sorry, you said state dinner so casually. But for you it must be.”

“I haven’t been to that many.” Not the best argument on my part.

Geoffrey arches an eyebrow. “More than five?”

I warm. He’s got me there. “But less than ten.”

He laughs again, and this time I join him, happy to be on the inside of the joke. With him.

“It’s not too far out of your world either. You’re the one who wrote Cooper Grant’s biography. I know you must have accompanied him to those kinds of events.”

He lightly touches the base of the wineglass, absentmindedly. “It’s different though. I was there for work, not among peers.” His tone is wistful, and I wonder if more is there.

“Do you like that kind of writing?”

“To be honest? No. I did it for the paycheck and the hope that it would be a bestseller.”

“That paid off. Went to number one on the *Times*.”

He nods. “For three weeks, until the Britney Spears memoir knocked it off. And rightfully so, she deserved it.”

I grin before taking another sip of my wine. “I’m sure you have tons of offers for those kinds of projects now. Would you do another one?”

“Depends on who’s asking. Book writing is hell, especially when your subject has a very particular view of how they want to be portrayed.”

It’s my turn to arch an eyebrow. “Sounds like there’s a story there. Tell me more.”

"Do you really want to know if those blind items about him are true?"

My eyes widen, knowing there's everything from secret love-child allegations to rumors that Cooper's broke. "Tell me." Playful, I lean forward, and Geoffrey does the same, as if he's about to let me in on a big secret.

He lowers his tone, a stage whisper. "I signed an NDA." He grins like the Cheshire Cat at my disappointment.

"You're a tease." Instinctively, I put my hand on his forearm as if to push him away, but he stops me. That same spark from earlier rears its head, but ten times as strong. He must feel it too and pulls me closer instead. What started off as a teasing gesture turns into something charged, dangerous.

Almost all of the space between us is gone now. I can hear Geoffrey's breathing, at pace with mine, in and out with shallow, measured exhalations. This close, I can see flecks of brown in his eyes, and I wonder if they're more hazel than green. He glances down at my mouth, and I bite my bottom lip from the nerves of it all.

Our gazes connect again, and the look in his eyes asks the question. I'm not sure if it's him or me who answers it, but one of us closes the distance, and our lips touch. Mine are fuller, but his are no less warm and soft. He brushes his tongue against my bottom lip, hesitant at first, and my whole body inches toward him. When I open my mouth, it's with urgency, but he keeps kissing me languidly, as if we have all the time in the world.

He moves a hand at the nape of my neck and gently

angles his body so that I can lean more into him. I haven't felt this, the sensation of being close to another person, in so long that I sigh audibly, and he pulls me tighter in response. To be held so completely and fully after all this time without it—it's dizzying.

I don't know how long we kiss, but we do so without pause, our mouths returning to each other over and over, as if we both fear that once we stop, we'll know better than to start again. Despite everything in my body telling me not to, I'm the one to break away first. We're both panting. His eyes are wild, and his pupils are huge. The expression on his face is a mixture of regret and wanting. I'm sure I look the same. I get up, needing distance between us before I speak. "We can't do that again." My voice is shaking.

He rubs both of his hands over his face in a gesture of frustration. "I know."

"It was a mistake."

He looks up at me, and I see the flicker of hurt in his eyes, but he nods his head. "It was deeply unprofessional. It won't happen again. I'll go." His words are reasonable, they're the *right* thing to say, but still, they land like a blow to my chest.

When he gets up and gathers his things, I watch him with my mind racing. When I speak again, it's to his back. I can't bear to look at his face right now for fear of losing my resolve. "It can't happen again because I can't think about the kind of person that makes me. Someone who moves on so quickly from the love of my life."

I don't wait for his response before I flee to my bedroom. I leave him there in my living room, knowing he'll be gone when I get back. The thought of his absence mixes with the lust and guilt that's swirling inside of me, and I can't tell which is causing the hurt.

VII

I wake up the next morning to an email from Geoffrey with Wendy cc'd.

Hi Ndidi,

I won't be at the office to shadow today and tomorrow. I'll be back by the end of the week.

—Geoffrey

I let out a sigh, equal parts regret and relief that I don't have to face him for a few days, but getting out of bed is still a struggle. Now that I'm conscious, the kiss replays on a loop in my head.

I check the clock, see that it's 7:10 a.m. Adamma's time. She might already be with a patient, but I FaceTime her anyway.

She answers from her office, dressed in the Saint Laurent blazer I gave her for Christmas last year. She has on her chunky black frames that she thinks make her look older and wiser, more like what she imagines a therapist should be.

"What's going on?" She skips the pleasantries, able to read me in the less than two seconds we've been on this call.

"I kissed Geoffrey last night." I say it in a rush, knowing the only way I'll get it out is if I do it quickly.

"What?" She's surprised, not her usual measured self. I can't tell if her reaction is to what I did or that I told her.

"I had a horrible day at work, and he was supposed to interview me in the evening. I wanted to get out of the office, so I invited him back to the house. One thing led to another, and we kissed."

Her face scrunches up in confusion, and I know we've crossed over from "professional health-care provider Adamma" to "younger sister calling out my bullshit" mode. "There's got to be a little more to it than 'one thing led to another.' Please elaborate."

I sink back into the pillows, knowing they will partially obscure my face. "He was asking a lot of questions about OneK and the fact that I never worked there."

She nods. "And?"

"To make me more comfortable, he suggested that we trade question for question. It started off light . . . but I don't know. It got more personal, and I felt like I was seeing who he was as a person, not just a journalist: A bit tough on himself, hardworking. Thinks of himself as an outsider, ever since he was little. There's just this warmth to him that came through."

"Sounds like someone else I know." I smile, knowing she's right. The ways we're alike aren't lost on me either. "But those are all good qualities, Didi."

"I know. And he's also so perceptive. And kind. I feel so comfortable around him, despite the fact he's a journalist."

Adamma laughs. "I think it's OK to trust someone until they give you a reason not to."

"I also told him stuff about me that I don't usually share." Her eyebrows raise, and I backtrack. "Just about growing up. And I told him about the starter-wife incident." Adamma's the one other person who knows that story.

"How did he react?"

"Outraged on my behalf."

"The only correct response."

"OK, Miss Therapist. I thought all emotional responses are valid?"

"Not when it comes to racism." We both laugh, and I kick the comforter off my legs. She's quiet for a moment, and I can see her wheels turning. "Sounds like you let your guard down. Felt safe enough to kiss him?"

"I wouldn't say that safety was what I felt in that moment." I bite my lip. Adamma doesn't know the truth about my involvement in OneK. It's the only secret I've kept from her, and I shut that information away so long ago that I haven't interrogated my subterfuge in years. "I was on edge." It's all I can bring myself to say. "But the kiss felt inevitable, like it had to happen."

She keeps her face neutral, but I know she's processing. "'Inevitable'? OK, that's a big word. How does he make you feel?"

"Does that matter right now? Since it happened, the only feeling I can really access is guilt over the whole situation."

Adamma gives me the look. The one Black moms everywhere have perfected, the one that says, *Don't you dare lie to me.* "I'm not in a place to tell you what your feelings are, but do you really think that's true?"

I bury my face further into a pillow so that my voice is muffled. "No."

"Girl, you're gonna smother yourself."

I groan, but I sit up. "Guilt isn't the only thing I feel. In the moment, I felt so many things. Need. Terror. Excitement. Giddiness. Newness." If I'm completely honest, it was one of the best kisses of my life. But something in me holds back from saying that out loud. I'm betraying Alex's memory enough as it is.

"You felt all of those things, so why is guilt the only feeling you're willing to validate?"

"Isn't it the most important one? Alex has been gone for a little over a year; what kind of wife am I if I'm already catching feelings for someone else?" Even though I know I'm not still married, it's hard to stop feeling that way. Unlike a divorce, losing a partner to death isn't a choice. There was no process to uncouple ourselves, one that gave time and space for me to think about myself as a single woman. Until now, I've only thought of myself as alone.

"It means you're human. There's no one-size-fits-all timeline to moving on after your spouse dies."

"Tell that to the Victorians."

"Didi, I know you think you should feel a certain way right now, but I want you to focus on how you actually feel. Maybe it's a one-time thing, or maybe it could be something more."

"Well, there's his job to consider. I wouldn't want him to jeopardize his work over this." I realize how true the statement is as soon as it leaves my mouth. He's amazing at what he does, but the ethics of any entanglement with a subject are pretty murky.

"That's valid. But it's something you could figure out down the road, if your connection with him becomes important. What if you just let yourself feel your feelings without assigning labels to them?"

"And then what?"

"And then you can decide what's important and go from there." She sounds so reasonable, and I'm struck by how unfair it is that Adamma inherited all the emotional stability.

"All right. I'll try as much as I'm able to." We both know pushing down my feelings is one of the things I excel most at in life. A bad coping mechanism, learned early and perfected over time.

"Do you think Alex would want you to spend the rest of your life alone?"

I usually hate it when people evoke Alex's name when it comes to things he can no longer weigh in on, but Adamma says it so gently, it stops me in my tracks. We had our fair share of ups and downs before he died, but I know at the core of it all, we still wanted the best for each other. I don't answer, preferring to think of it as a rhetorical question.

Adamma has a meeting to get to, so we say our good-byes and hang up.

I roll onto my stomach and close my eyes with my face pressed into the pillows. Part of me wants to take the day off and stay in bed, but I force myself up. Instead of getting dressed, I put on my swimsuit. I haven't reestablished my London swimming routine since I got back to the U.S., but I need to get out of my head today.

The ache of propelling myself through water for an hour brings me back into my body and mellows out my mind, and when I'm done, I'm calm enough to sit poolside and actually think about what I'm feeling. I absentmindedly brush my hand over my mouth as if I can still capture the sensation of Geoffrey's lips on mine. He makes me feel like I could desire things again, and that's scary. I've had a lot of time to think about what I want to do with my life this year, but I've been so focused on the foundation and getting rid of the money that my personal life has been a footnote. I don't know if I'm ready to consider what it could look like. Who it could be with. And now one kiss has me ready to shut it down completely.

By the time I put on a shift dress and get ready to go into the office, I see that I have a message from Geoffrey. We've texted a bit here and there about logistics, but this time, I know it's nothing that mundane.

Geoffrey: Just wanted to check in and say that if you're uncomfortable, I don't have to complete this piece. It would be a disappointment not to write this story, but say the word and I'm gone.

Those last two words send a chill through me. The past year, I've associated them with Alex, since it's the polite way people speak of his death. Geoffrey leaving is nowhere near as final, but given how my body responded, I know I'd still experience his absence as a loss. And practically, there's the article to consider and the good it would do for the foundation. Also, there's him. His work and his wants.

Ndidi: We can put it behind us. I know it doesn't always seem like it, but I've enjoyed working with you. I wouldn't want to lose that.

Or lose you, I think. But I can't write that. Adamma's reminder to let myself feel everything pops into my head just as his text ellipsis appears on the screen. Then disappears. Then reappears again after what feels like an eternity passes. In other words, about three minutes.

Geoffrey: I've enjoyed working on this story as well. Looking forward to continuing it.

So professional and straightforward, though some small and awful part of me hopes that there's subtext to that "continuing it." Not that I would act on it again. Either way, his response doesn't warrant a reply, so I place my phone into my bag and go meet Bill at the car. Right now, every decision at the foundation is fraught, and I cannot get distracted.

As Bill pulls up to the office, I push Geoffrey and the kiss out of my mind.

VIII

Ten days later, Bill drops Wendy and me off at Chavez Elementary, a school where the majority of the kids are reading below grade level and many are English-as-a-second-language learners. It's our first company volunteer day, where we get out of the office and meet with one of our orgs in person—Elijah's idea, a way to keep in touch with the human impact of our work. We've been giving away roughly half a million a day, which is so much money it's almost impossible to conceptualize. We're hoping these quarterly field trips help. There's a small team of us here from the foundation: Elijah, Wendy, Simone, myself, and Geoffrey, who is here as a volunteer, not a writer.

Geoffrey returned back on-site a week ago, but I've successfully avoided being alone in the same space as him. He's sat in on all the group meetings, which is unnerving but tolerable. He sent me some questions about the Safe Syringes harm-reduction center we're supporting, but I referred him to Elijah. And any time I've needed to get work done, I've hidden out on the couch in Wendy's office. I knew I couldn't dodge him forever, but it was working. Until today.

According to Wendy, he heard the team talking about the outing and offered to join. He's clearly the more mature person in this equation.

Geoffrey holds the school doors open for everyone, and as I pass through them, I decide to stop being a coward. "Thanks for coming today. You certainly didn't have to."

He shrugs like it's no big deal. "I had a free morning. And I'm meeting up with a buddy nearby tonight."

"I didn't know you had a friend in town." I don't know why I would know that, but it feels like I should.

"Yeah, Martin. He's a retired photographer. I've known him since we were both wet behind the ears. He owns a bar now."

"Any place I'd know?"

"I doubt it, unless shitty dive bars are your thing?"

"They could be."

If the look of surprise on his face is any indication, it comes out flirtier than I intended. I'm saved from having to backpedal when Janet Young, the head of the reading club, greets us at the cafeteria doors. "Who's ready to get their hands dirty?"

I've spoken to her a few times on the phone, so it's nice to put a face to a voice. She's a retired teacher in her sixties with red shoulder-length hair, the energy of someone half her age, and grip strength that makes me question my workout routine.

"We're so glad to have y'all here today!" Janet goes down the line introducing herself to the team, and I see Geoffrey do a double take after their handshake. I catch his eye. We both grin, and he wags his hand as if she did some real damage. It's a goofy gesture, but it makes me feel like things are OK between us. And reminds me that I do like having him around. Then Janet claps her hands like a camp counselor to get our attention and snaps me out of that thought.

"All right, let's circle up while I give you folks the rundown." Janet has a deep Southern twang I don't hear too much in this area, but it fits with her "all are welcome" vibe. We gather around her, and I find myself shoulder to shoulder with Geoffrey. I ignore the spiciness of his cologne, musky and warm with a hint of citrus, and the slight uptick in my heartbeat.

Janet breaks down the day for us: We'll either read aloud to the youngest kids or do tutoring sessions with the older ones. Then we'll do a craft. "I'll need four of you to partner up and decide which grade you wanna work with, and the fifth person to volunteer here with me."

Elijah steps forward. "I love kids in theory, from afar. I'd love to stick with you, Janet, if that's OK."

Before I can claim Wendy, she grabs Simone's arm. "Let's take the big kids. I fear my energy isn't up for the little ones." I try to make eye contact with Wendy, to give her a bit of a *What the fuck?* look, but she's zeroed in on Janet. Part of me wonders if she picked up on something between Geoffrey and me. It would be classic Wendy to maneuver this so I have to face my problems instead of ignoring them.

Geoffrey lightly bumps his shoulder against mine. It's a

slight move, but I'm warm at the point of contact. "Looks like we're with the littles then." There's a hesitation in his voice, like he senses I might back out of working with him. We're here to help though.

I muster up as much pep in my voice as I can manage. "Let's do this."

"Vámonos, mijo. This is our stop." Geoffrey reads from *Julián Is a Mermaid* in a gruff but feminine tone as he performs the grandmother character. He's good at it, and I'm impressed. My nephew tells me to skip the voices whenever I attempt them.

"Do it again!" one of the kids yells, and Geoffrey obliges. If he's as exhausted as I am by working with six very adorable, very antsy five-year-olds, he doesn't show it.

Elma, a girl who clearly has artsy parents judging by her outfit, keeps looking at me. I can't make out the expression on her face, somewhere between curious and hostile. I smile at her and whisper, "Do you not like the story?"

"I've heard it before." Her eyes dart to Geoffrey, then back at me. "Is he your husband?" Of course, she says it loud enough that Geoffrey and the other kids hear. Everyone's attention turns to me.

"No, he's not. Why don't we get back to the story?"

"Good idea, so—" Geoffrey starts.

But Elma isn't having it. "If he's not your husband, is he

your boyfriend? My mom has a boyfriend, but she wants him to postpone."

"Postpone what?" I ask her.

"I think you mean propose," Geoffrey chimes in, helpful as ever.

"*Pro-pose.*" Elma drags the word out, getting a feel for it. "Are you going to propose?" This time she directs the question at Geoffrey.

"No, Ms. Ndidi and I aren't boyfriend and girlfriend."

"Why not?"

"Because we work together. Let's get back to Julián." Geoffrey picks the book back up and points to a beautiful illustration of the main character wearing a mermaid tail made out of a curtain.

But Elma's got more thoughts. "My mom met her boyfriend at work. She said that's the best place to find a man."

I bite back my laughter as I wonder what conversations this girl is overhearing and whether her mother is aware of it. There's a slight flush to Geoffrey's face that wasn't there before.

He clears his throat. "That's good for your mom, but we're just here to read to you guys. Why don't we all take a little wiggle break before we get back to reading?" All the kids, including Elma, jump up and run to the designated play area. I'm the last to get up, and Geoffrey holds out a hand to help me.

"I'm not that old yet," I say but take his hand anyway.

"I'm from the South. It's kind of in my DNA to help a lady."

"You forget I am too. I know all about Southern gentlemen, and I know that most of it is bullshit."

"Can't argue with you there." He's still holding my hand even though I'm on my feet. I have that feeling I get when I stand up too fast, when all the blood rushes to my head. Before I can think about it too much, one of the boys starts zooming toward us.

"AHHHHH!!!!!" A collective yelp from the kids brings the room to a new level of chaos.

Geoffrey lets go of my hand, and I brush my palms against my jeans. "Looks like they started without us. Lead the way, Captain Wiggle."

"Who's ready?" Geoffrey leads us in shaking our limbs high, low, fast, and slow. The kids eat it up, squealing, suggesting their own commands. He makes silly faces and noises as we move, and I'm grinning despite myself.

After a minute or two, we resettle on the carpet, and it's my turn to read. This time, Elma snuggles into my side, wanting to get the best view of the pictures. Geoffrey and I make our way through the book a total of four times, swapping back and forth as we go. Janet warned us that the kids would demand multiple reads; something about the repetition soothes them. *Me too*, I think. By the time we get to the craft—decorating the tails of cut-out mermaids—the kids are quieter and more focused. The hour and a half flies by. A volunteer swings by to grab our kids for dismissal, and Geoffrey and I are left alone to reset the classroom. We work in silence, hanging the chairs upside down on the desks. It's comfortable.

"You're really good with kids," I tell him, my voice more tender than I mean it to be.

"Thanks. I don't get much of a chance to be around them. Mostly when I visit my sister and her foursome."

I let out a whistle at the number. "Four?"

"Yup. And it was planned too." Like he knew that was the follow-up question I was too polite to ask. "She's been a nurturer since we were kids. Always did her best to take care of me when my mom was at work and we were on our own."

"Still, I can't even imagine. Adamma, my sister, has one, and she's thinking about a second. But Jalen's already five, so I'll be surprised if it happens."

"You never know. Lindsey's first three were all two years apart. Four years went by before she decided to have the last one."

Geoffrey turns his back to me, erasing errant scribbles on the whiteboard.

I stoop down to the floor to pick up the little bits of scrap paper from our cutouts. "Alex and I thought about kids, but becoming a parent was never something either of us was particularly called to." I wasn't planning on sharing this, but I find the words tumbling out of my mouth.

I'm surprised that I feel compelled to tell him more. "He was so committed to his work, and I knew that if we got pregnant, I'd be parenting alone. That wasn't something I wanted. Neither was becoming one of those people who hire nannies to do most of the work. I mean, no judgment, but that's not what I'd want."

I'd never actually, explicitly shared that line of thinking with Alex. He just knew that I wasn't interested in having kids. If he had really wanted them, I could have been convinced. Maybe in another life. But I'm glad it wasn't this one—I don't want to think about how much more difficult this past year would have been with children to consider. A visible, constant reminder of who we lost.

"No judgment, huh? Maybe a little judgment?" Geoffrey is stooped down on the floor beside me, picking up crafting debris along with me, and I can see the glimmer in his eyes.

"Just a little."

He laughs at my deadpan tone. We both reach for the same strip of paper, and our hands brush. This isn't even the first time we've touched today, but I'm starting to feel like a character in a Jane Austen novel. Flummoxed. It's a bit ridiculous. I retract my hand and let him grab the scrap.

"Sounds like you made the best decision for yourself."

"I think I did. And what about you?" I ask, wanting to tug us back into the "one for you, one for me" game.

"I've never even been close to thinking about having kids. I enjoy them, but I don't have the desire to be responsible for one. Love being the fun uncle."

"Today definitely made that clear. Your wiggle dancing was inspired."

"Glad I had the opportunity to showcase my skills. I should make it more of a priority to volunteer with an organization like this."

"You should when you have the time. But do you ever have free time?"

He shakes his head. "Nah. I'm away from home so much that when I'm back, it's playing catch-up. General life-maintenance stuff but also with my friends, joining in with whatever they have going on with their spouses and kids. I find myself at a lot of recitals and games."

"You find where you fit into other people's lives," I say, certain it's true.

He nods slowly. "Something like that." The way he's looking at me now is curious, like maybe I saw too much.

I throw the last pile of paper scraps into the trash can. "The floor looks good. Proud of us. I think we're all done here." We both stand up at the same time, and we're face-to-face, a little too close for comfort.

Geoffrey clears his throat. "Are you busy after this?"

I shake my head no, uncertain where this is leading.

"Would you want to grab a drink with me at my friend Martin's bar? He'll be working, and I'd welcome the company while he's busy."

"Do you, uh, think that's a good idea?"

"We don't have any more interviews scheduled. I have enough to move on to other sources now, so . . ." He says it like he's convincing himself as much as he's convincing me. The logical part of my brain knows his reasoning is flimsy, but—

"Plus, we're friends, right?" When he asks me, his face is so hopeful it cracks my heart just a bit.

"Friends." If that's what we're calling having a raging crush on someone. "Friends who can grab a drink together. Yeah, I'd like that."

He lifts his right eyebrow, and I wonder exactly how much trouble I'm getting myself into.

IX

"Where is this place?" We've been walking for what must be ten minutes now, down a side street in NoPa I'm not familiar with. I stop to look around, feeling like a stranger in my own city.

"You'll see." Geoffrey grins and keeps leading the way. There's an unfamiliar part of me that realizes I'll follow him anywhere. Geoffrey turns a corner, and we're standing in front of a tiny, hole-in-the-wall bar called The Alibi.

"Are you sure you want me to meet him?" The question slips out, and the answer feels more important than it has any right to.

Geoffrey looks down, puts his hands into his jeans' pockets, and shrugs his shoulders. The move is boyish in a way I haven't seen from him before. I feel myself smiling. "He always wants to know about the people I think are interesting."

I know Geoffrey's just trying to say the right thing, to stick to what we agreed to, but it doesn't stop the pang in my heart when I hear him say that there's nothing more to this outing.

Geoffrey holds the door open for me, and we're met

with a burst of noise: clinking glasses, patrons shouting over the lo-fi hip-hop playing in the background. The place is homey without feeling rundown, cool without feeling like it's trying too hard. There's a tall Black man with shoulder-length locks tied up in a low bun and his back to us, helping a customer close his tab. He's wearing a distressed gray T-shirt that could either be worthless or cost five hundred dollars.

Geoffrey walks us over to the bar. "Ten pickleback shots and a screwdriver, please."

The bartender whips around. "Only if you want hell and back again." It's clear this is some inside joke between the two of them because Geoffrey pulls him into a bear hug. I'm struck by how much love there is between them. When they pull apart, Geoffrey fans a hand between the two of us. "Martin Hargrove, meet Ndidi Davis."

"Does one of you want to fill me in on what 'ten pickleback shots and a screwdriver' means?" I can't keep the smirk off my face.

"I don't think she needs to hear that," Geoffrey says. But we grab stools at the corner of the bar, and Martin proceeds to tell me the story of how they first met anyway. Something about a drinking contest on the campaign trail with a rival reporting team, whoever won got first dibs on a sit-down with the presidential candidate. "Cue the two-day hangover," Martin concludes.

"Not our proudest moment," Geoffrey offers, looking pained.

"We were inseparable after that. But my journalism career was a lot shorter. I wasn't as serious about it as Geoffrey. I wasn't as good either."

"Yes, you were. All my stories' best photos were by you." There's a deep admiration between them.

Martin shrugs it off. "Takes a special breed." He moves behind the bar. "What're you drinking?"

I peruse the menu quickly before landing on a lambic sour. Geoffrey arches that eyebrow.

"What?" I sense that my smirk is back. Or never left.

"I'm just surprised. I mean, this is the woman who takes a cup of sugar in her coffee."

It's not lost on me that he remembers, but that's his job, isn't it? To clock small details. "Can't a woman contain multitudes?" I respond with faux outrage.

"Makes for a more interesting subject." He takes a long pull of his own beer, a pilsner, and I find my gaze glued to his lips before I catch myself. Good God, I need to chill. I dart my eyes away, but I can tell he caught me. He's fighting off a smile. He mutters something I can't make out over the noise.

"What was that?"

He starts to answer, but the smile slips off his face when he glances down at his phone. "My editor is blowing me up. I'll be back in a second."

Our shoulders brush as he gets up, and I note the shiver that runs through me. I watch him exit through the front door.

Martin sees me sitting alone and brings a stack of clean tumblers over to me. "I told him he couldn't bring his dates here to dine and dash anymore."

"Good thing I'm not a date. Just an interview subject."

Martin laughs, bright and open. "I don't want to overstep or make you uncomfortable, but in the fifteen years I've known Geoffrey, he's never brought 'an interview subject' to this bar."

That comment sends a little zing down my spine. The way he says "interview subject" like there's innuendo. "New era, I guess."

"I don't know about that. He's a creature of habit."

Unsure how to respond, I take another sip of my drink and look around. "It's a nice environment you've created here. Cozy and welcoming."

"Is that billionaire-speak for small?"

"You read right through me." I give him a wink for good measure.

He sets down the glass he's drying. "I can see why Geoffrey likes you."

The comment hits me right between the ribs. I know I should steer the conversation back to general niceties, but I also really don't want to. "Listen, we're just friends. But if I were to say we weren't . . . what do you think? Can I trust this?"

"You mean him?"

I nod, trying to keep my nerve.

He purses his lips, considering. "I think Geoffrey's a

really intentional, what-you-see-is-what-you-get kind of guy. If he brought you here, it means he's trying to let you in." Martin's words are exactly what I've hoped and feared: This could be real if we let it.

Geoffrey comes back, and I down the rest of my drink, which I'm sure makes me look guilty of . . . something. Geoffrey arches a brow at Martin, who throws his hands up in mock defense. "I've been on my best behavior. Another round?" Martin directs the question to the both of us, but from the way they both look at me, I know the ball is in my court.

"Sure, why not?" I say with more ease than I'm feeling. If this is real, that means something could go wrong, and someone could get hurt. That person could be Geoffrey; that person could be me.

"I'll get on that. Why don't y'all move to that booth over there? My regulars are about to come in, heavy drinkers who like to trauma dump to a nonjudgmental third party."

"Nonjudgmental and you in the same sentence?" Geoffrey gently ribs Martin.

"Keep it up if you don't want your drinks comped." We all laugh.

The Alibi is more crowded than before, and I find myself pushed closer to Geoffrey. He places a hand on my lower back to guide me to the booth, and the warmth of him there sparks an ember in my belly. I compose myself enough to keep walking and slip into the booth, which is smaller than it looks when Geoffrey slides in next to me.

His thigh presses against mine, and our closeness sets off mixed signals in my mind that I try to suppress. *We're friends, we're friends, we're friends*, I tell myself.

"How'd your call go?"

"My editor got a tip about Alexander Smit buying multiple properties in South Dakota of all places. It could be nothing, but it's something I'll have to monitor."

I shudder. "That guy gives me the creeps." He's a technocrat billionaire with some backward ideas about America's declining population and how to fix it.

"Have you met him?"

"Not really. We've been at some of the same parties, unfortunately, but Alex would always fake a work emergency if he tried to talk to us." I'm about to launch into the full story when Martin brings us our next round, and I swear he winks at Geoffrey before scurrying away.

"But anyway." He settles into the seat and, in doing so, shifts closer to me. His elbow knocks mine on the table. "Question for question?"

"I don't think we need that game anymore," I say, surprising Geoffrey and myself. "We can just talk." I realize I don't want this to feel anything like an interview.

He grins. "That's just fine." He drawls out the last word, and I hear the slightest hint of his Southern twang. It must come out when he's drinking, and I tuck that fact away in my mind.

He takes a sip of his drink. "What's your favorite movie?"

"If I want to cry, *In the Mood for Love*. If I want to laugh, *Clueless*."

"You really do contain multitudes."

I nudge his shoulder with mine. "How about you?"

"You want the respectable answer or the real one?"

"The real one, of course."

"*The Pirate.* It's an old Judy Garland and Gene Kelly musical. It's so corny, and there's probably something problematic in it, but it reminds me of watching old movies on TCM with my grandma—wanting to be somewhere else, to travel the world."

"That's sweet, I'll have to check it out."

"Please, don't. I'll lose any cool points I've accumulated."

"Who says you have any?" When he laughs, I sink into the moment: The simple pleasure of being a woman enjoying a conversation with a cute guy at a bar.

We exchange softball questions at a rapid-fire pace. I learn his favorite color is green even though he thinks it's silly to still have a favorite color. The Oasis reunion tour in London was the last concert he went to, and he agrees with Obama: People over the age of eight shouldn't eat ketchup. He learns that I speak Igbo and Spanish, that my favorite color is blue—always has been—and that I'm afraid of birds.

The conversation is loose and fun, the kind I haven't been a part of in God knows how long. We stray away from fun get-to-know-yous long enough for him to tell me that his grandma died before she could see him make it as a journalist, someone on the level of her beloved Andy Rooney. I tell him about Adamma's struggle to get pregnant and the bittersweet triumph of Jalen's birth after a loss. Somehow, these moments don't dampen the mood—they anchor me to the moment, and to the fact that I feel comfortable with Geoffrey.

At some point, he drapes his arm loosely on the back of the booth, almost around me but not quite. I don't move, feeling alive in the space between us.

Once we're three drinks in, Geoffrey's twang comes out in full force. I am making fun of how he pronounces "lawyer" like *LAW-yer* when Martin pops back to our table with a dish towel thrown over his shoulder and a tray of drinks he's busing. "Last call was an hour ago." He says it like he's caught us.

I look around and realize the place is completely empty. "Oh God, why didn't you kick us out earlier?" I jump up, not wanting to be in the way.

Geoffrey raises an eyebrow. "You didn't notice the bar shutting down around us?"

I warm, and I know it's not from the alcohol. Both men laugh. Martin punches Geoffrey's shoulder. "It's all good; I'm used to Geoffrey sitting with me while I close the bar."

"Well, thanks for allowing me to partake in the tradition."

"Anytime." Martin pulls me in for a hug. After a round of goodbyes, I order an Uber to get back home, something I haven't done since . . . I can't even remember. Geoffrey stands close to me, his proximity a shield from the night air. We're quiet as we wait, and it dawns on me that I've spent almost twelve hours with him today. And yet it felt like no time at all.

I sneak a peek at him and trace his profile with my

eyes. The jut of his brow, the slope of his nose, the perfect pink of his bottom lip. I want him to kiss me right now.

He turns and catches me staring. I want him to close the gap—I'm too nervous to do it myself—but instead he swallows, hard, and points across the street. "I think your car is here."

I break our gaze and check my phone to confirm. "I had a good time tonight. This was fun." I say it to the screen.

"Me too."

He pulls me in for a hug, and I'm surrounded by his scent, warm and spicy, with a hint of lemon underneath. I close my eyes and press my face into his chest, hoping he can feel how much tonight meant to me. I don't trust myself to put it into words. Instead, I tell him goodnight, and we break apart. I walk toward my car, and I can feel his eyes on me. But I don't dare look back.

X

"What do you mean you can't come tonight?" I pace around my bedroom on the phone with Wendy, who has just informed me she's skipping the gala.

"I think one of those fifth graders gave me something. There was one little boy who couldn't stop coughing in my face." To her credit, her voice does sound hoarse.

"I'm sorry you're sick." I hate to be that person who only thinks of themselves, but I also want to know if it's too late for me to back out. "I don't like to go to these things, Wendy, and especially not by myself." I sigh. It was always easier to do with Alex, when I could just be the wife, not the person signing the big check.

"You're their unofficial guest of honor. Of course you have to go." Wendy's tone is enough to make me pull my head out of my ass. Of course I have to go.

"You're right, you're right. I wonder if I can get someone to be my plus-one this late." I run through a list of names, but a last-minute gala invitation isn't something you can exactly spring on someone with no notice. It's not like I've done the best job keeping up relationships in the last year, even since I've been back in town. When did my life become so small?

"Oh, I already asked Geoffrey to go with you."

For the first time in my life, my jaw actually drops. "As in Geoffrey Campbell?"

"Yes. They were very selective about the press for the party, so we couldn't get him on the list in a professional capacity. It seemed like a good way to get him access."

"He wants to come?" My heart races at the thought of seeing Geoffrey again so soon. I'm not sure I'm strong enough to fight the momentum we built last night.

"It'll be a good scene for the profile." Wendy says it like this is the most logical, straightforward thing. "Or I could call Henry if you want? He's already going; you can tag along with him and his wife."

"You don't need to threaten me." I'm somewhere between joking and serious, and she knows it.

"Good. Geoffrey it is."

I can't argue with Wendy, who knows that the exhaustion of schmoozing alone would send me to bed for a week. Alex came alive at these kinds of events, which always surprised me. Not many programmers thrive in the spotlight, but he did. People used to speculate that he'd run for office later in life. I never asked him directly, but if the right opportunity came along, I'm certain he would have considered it.

I couldn't see myself as a politician's wife, but like so many things with Alex, if he asked me to, I would have figured it out. I'd channel Michelle Obama, whose sense of duty was stronger than her own self-preservation. A character trait I find as admirable as it is heartbreaking. And deeply familiar.

But that was the past, and instead, I'll be the one everyone's eyes are on tonight. Wendy keeps me on the phone to go over the guest list, and when we hang up, I have a text from Geoffrey.

Geoffrey: Hope you don't mind having me as your impromptu date tonight. Just say the word if you'd rather go solo.

Part of me wants to take the out, but a larger part of me thinks I need to stop worrying so much about things that haven't, and quite possibly won't, happen. I take a few deep breaths and type my response.

Ndidi: I'd be honored to have you as Replacement Wendy.

Geoffrey: First Captain Wiggle, now Replacement Wendy. What do you have against my government name?

His words make me smile, and I'm brought back to how flirtatious the conversation got between us last night. It's one thing in a crowded bar, but it feels more intentional now.

Geoffrey: Replacement Wendy is a high bar for me to live up to.
Ndidi: I promise not to hold you to her standards.
Geoffrey: And I'll try not to disappoint.

I completely missed online dating, and flirting over text is new for me, especially with someone I'm just getting to know.

Geoffrey's texts should be platonic, professional. And I should be interpreting them that way, not acting like a high schooler who's hoping my crush will invite me to prom. I throw my phone onto the bed and flop back against the pillows anyway.

"Why am I like this?" I say out loud just to get the thought out of my mind.

I step into my Cult Gaia Renata dress, a fringed navy halter gown that the stylist I sometimes work with forced me to try on despite my fear that it was made for a woman half my age. It has a low back and a slit up the skirt. It's outside of my usual wheelhouse, but it shows off my toned shoulders—thank you, swimming—and the color looks good against my skin. The stylist was right.

I'm no clotheshorse, but I learned the hard way that hiring a professional is a worthy investment. The photos of me in an ill-fitting bustier at an Oprah party still make me shudder in embarrassment.

I've been wearing my hair in bohemian braids down to my mid-back to protect my natural hair, and my hairstylist pinned them into a soft updo for the event. I always do my makeup myself—I know a soft, neutral eye and a glossy lip never fail me, and I find the process relaxing. I throw on a pair of dangly earrings and decide to stop there.

I take myself in from multiple angles through the mirrors in my closet. I know I look good. I'm going to need this confidence boost to fully and publicly own my new role: Ndidi Davis, philanthropist. And Ndidi Davis, widow. Who may or may not be going on her first date with Geoffrey Campbell.

XI

Bill pulls the car up to the Hibernia, one of my favorite event venues in the city. It's a historic bank that survived the great earthquake and fire of 1906 that nearly destroyed the whole city. Ornate Beaux-Arts architecture and Tiffany-style skylights make it feel like being transported to another time. I offered Geoffrey a ride, but he said he'd meet me here instead.

There's a small line of cars ahead of us, and Bill maneuvers to the designated drop-off area. I watch the valets assisting people, but when my door opens, I see Geoffrey instead, looking devastatingly handsome in a black tuxedo. My jaw drops again as he offers me his hand.

I try to recover. "I didn't know you were moonlighting as a valet."

"One of the many skills I keep under wraps." Geoffrey's grasp is firm as he helps me out of the backseat. He drinks me up, taking in every detail of my outfit. I shiver, feeling everywhere his eyes land on me: The "V" of satin at my neck, the hug of the dress across my hips. He opens his mouth to say something but then closes it. Opens it again. I've never seen a human reboot before, but now I know what it looks like. Can't say I mind it. "You look incredible," Geoffrey finally manages.

"Thank you. You don't look too bad yourself. How'd you get a tux on such short notice? I can't imagine that was in your travel bag."

He brushes off a faux piece of dirt on his lapel. "A guy likes to keep some mysteries to himself."

"I feel like you'll tell me before the night's end."

"We'll see." We both smile before I realize we're holding up traffic.

I reach to place my hand on his arm, but then I notice the photographers by the entrance and think better of it. I'm not front-page-news material, but I'm not exactly a nobody. It's better to keep things on the conservative side. "Alex Davis's Widow Steps Out with a New Man Only a Year After His Death!" Not something I need to see in *Page Six* tomorrow.

I walk beside him instead, close but not close enough for it to mean anything. If Geoffrey notices my hesitation, he doesn't comment. When we arrive at the step-and-repeat, he makes a smooth exit so that I can take photos alone.

I'm not proud that everything I know about red-carpet posing comes from a TikTok influencer I fell down a rabbit hole with during the pandemic. Alex had considered investing in the app back when it was mostly a lip-synching platform. But there was no clear way to monetize it, and it had a limited audience at the time, so he passed. When it became the next big thing, he was pissed that he missed the opportunity. And in the meantime, I got addicted and learned that posing with a hand on my hip is called "the teapot" and is peak millennial cringe.

The step-and-repeat is quick and painless, and Geoffrey's waiting for me on the other side. We enter the main ballroom together. Circular tables are covered in white linens with peach peonies, white roses, and eucalyptus in the centerpieces. A couple hundred guests mingle while servers offer passed appetizers. I thought my nerves had dissipated, but they come back full force now that I'm inside with Geoffrey. I'm grateful I already ate because there's never enough food at these things.

"How many people do you know here?" Geoffrey asks me.

"Apart from you and Henry? I'd say I've met about thirty, and I actually know zero."

"Not your usual crowd?"

I shake my head, swiping two flutes of champagne off a server's tray and handing one to Geoffrey. "No, I'm horrible with names. And meeting people. More Alex's domain than mine."

"But it's yours now." He holds out his glass for us to clink. I comply, even though celebratory isn't exactly my mood.

"If it isn't Didi Davis!" At the sound of my name, both Geoffrey and I turn to see Henry walking over with Oscar Gómez in tow. Henry's eyebrows raise in surprise at the sight of Geoffrey next to me. I realize how close together we were standing and take a half step away. Henry introduces me to Oscar, whom I've only talked to over Zoom. He's the head of Homeless Health Care SF.

"Didn't expect to see you tonight, Campbell." Henry looks back and forth between the two of us.

"Geoffrey did me a favor. Wendy couldn't make it."

"Sorry to hear that, I was looking forward to meeting her in person. She writes one hell of an email," Oscar says with clear admiration.

"I'll be sure to tell her. Oscar, this is Geoffrey Campbell."

Oscar's face brightens in recognition. "The journalist?"

Geoffrey nods. "Guilty as charged."

"Oh man, that piece you wrote on privatized health care and insurance scams is a must-read for our new staffers."

"Well, Campbell is writing a piece about the work we're doing." Henry throws an arm around my shoulder, and it takes everything in me not to flinch.

Geoffrey frowns, sensing my discomfort. "I'm grateful Ndidi is letting me tell her story. It's been interesting to watch how she's building Giga Giving from the ground up."

"Yeah, it really is a team effort." Henry's smile falters as I slide out from under his arm.

Geoffrey nods. "Ndidi and Wendy did a great job selecting everyone."

I laugh but quickly cover my mouth, pretending I'm coughing. I normally hate this kind of dick-measuring contest, but it's funny to see Henry so out of sorts.

Oscar beams at me. "Your generosity has already made an impact. It looks like we'll be able to open a new harm-reduction center in the next year. Seriously, it means the world to us."

"I'm glad to hear it." Praise for doing the right thing makes me itchy. I down the rest of my drink and hold up the empty flute. "Think I'll head to the bar. Geoffrey?"

We excuse ourselves and join the line.

"You think Henry calls me Campbell because he forgot my first name?" Geoffrey inches slightly closer to me now that we're in the fray.

I laugh. "I think sounding like a Little League coach is the only way he feels comfortable performing his masculinity."

"Give me the real answer: Why'd you put him on your board? It's clear you don't get along."

I sigh. "Alex saw him as a mentor because he's older, and Henry gave him some free advice early on about how to structure OneK. Henry had made his first millions at the time but didn't invest in the app."

"So, he missed the windfall?"

"Correct. Always had regrets about that, I suspect. Don't get me wrong, the guy is still rich, but not as rich as he'd like to be. He wanted to work with Alex on something new, but they never had a chance."

I pause, not sure about sharing the rest. "Alex was actually on his way to meet up with him when his car was hit. At the funeral, Henry told me it wasn't fair that something as mundane as a car accident took someone so extraordinary. I agree with him about that, at least."

Geoffrey takes it all in. "I see why you brought him on."

"A bit of trauma bonding goes a long way." It's our turn to order, and I ask for two Manhattans. I hold mine up. "Let's have a good night." We clink again.

XII

The conversation with Henry turns out to be the worst of the night. It's easier than I thought it would be to make small talk and give big smiles with Geoffrey's calming presence by my side. If anything, people are just as interested in him as they are in me. After talking to the third man who's asked about the Cooper Grant book, Geoffrey pulls me aside to take a break at a well-hidden table in the corner. We end up playing a game of I Spy with the guests. For a party benefiting the homeless, there are an egregious number of Rolexes.

There's a special irony to giving money to charity while spending even more on your accessories, and it's not lost on anyone in attendance that to be taken seriously by this crowd means casually flaunting your wealth. I know this. And I know that as long as Giga is functional, I will have to play along.

It's my turn to come up with an object for him to guess, and I'm stuck between tennis bracelets or the lone fur stole I see when I spot Henry making introductions for an older woman wearing a necklace featuring a pear-shaped rock that would rival even the Taylor–Burton Diamond. Henry's head swivels, scanning the ballroom, and I get the feeling he's looking for me. Geoffrey gives me a sidelong glance. "You wanna get some fresh air?"

"You couldn't have better timing."

"On my count, we head for that door." He points to one in the opposite corner.

"You think it has an alarm?"

He shrugs. "Only one way to find out." Geoffrey looks over at Henry, whose back is to us. "One, two, three, let's go." Before I can fully comprehend what's happening, he takes off on a brisk walk toward the exit. And for the second time in twenty-four hours, I decide I'll follow this man anywhere.

Geoffrey pushes through the door just as I catch up. The alarm doesn't go off. It opens into a stairwell, and Geoffrey grins down at me from a few steps ahead.

"You knew that wouldn't go off."

He smirks. "I may have used my journalistic observational skills and noticed a few people sneak out this way."

"You could have told me." There's no heat behind my assertion, just a fondness I feel growing every time I'm around him. We end up on the rooftop we're not supposed to have access to. Other than a little cluster of the waitstaff vaping on one side, we're on our own. We stand by the dome, looking out onto the city.

"Y'know," I tell Geoffrey, "I was dreading coming tonight. But you did a pretty good job as Replacement Wendy."

"Only 'pretty good'? Where did I need improvement?" He shifts his gaze to me with a small smirk.

I pretend to think it over. "She would have given me more talking points for that guy from the mayor's office."

Geoffrey shakes his head. "You were a natural. Didn't need them."

"Really? I felt like it was obvious I was scrambling for things to say."

"See, this is something I've noticed about you. You're so good at lifting up others, but you downplay your own skills a lot."

My first instinct is to brush his comment off. But I know he's right, and something about him makes me want to stop turning away from uncomfortable truths. "It feels like a reflex at this point."

"You've always been like this?"

I pause, searching for the truth. Have I? For as long as I can remember. Since living here, at least. "Pretty much." I look across Market Street. "But you're right that it doesn't serve me. Probably hasn't for a very long time. If ever."

Geoffrey nods. "Good." His eyes crinkle like he's pleased to be standing next to me as I have this minirevelation. "And I'm glad you're having a good time. I am too."

"Did I say I was?" I gently tease him.

"I can read between the lines."

"Nothing gets past you." I raise my brows at him and take a sip of my cocktail. "I don't remember the last time I had this much fun at one of these events." I pause, giving myself the chance to draw inward again. Then proceeding anyway. "It makes me sad."

"Since Alex, you mean?"

"Even with him." It's a heavy truth, one I wasn't planning on talking about. But if I know anything by now, it's that I can't keep these truths from spilling out around Geoffrey Campbell. He waits for me to say more. He's dangerously good at staying quiet. His eyes are warm and encouraging, and I feel the steadying force of the foundation of trust we've already managed to build.

"We'd grown apart in those last couple of years together." I can't look at him when I say this. It feels almost traitorous.

"Did something happen?"

"Yes and no. There was nothing big. No infidelity, midlife crisis or anything. We just grew apart. He was so concerned about finding the next big app or tech development to get involved with. He had sold OneK years before, and I think he was restless."

Geoffrey nods. "A lot of entrepreneurs are like that. You strike gold once, and it becomes a challenge to do it again. To prove that you're the driver of your success and it wasn't just some perfect circumstance, some combination of timing and luck the first time around."

"Exactly. He acted like he had something to prove, and I just wasn't a part of that, and couldn't help him. Not that I had all that much going on. Which was kind of the problem."

"In what way?"

"Alex and I . . ." I shift in my shoes, leaning into the discomfort of being in heels for hours instead of the discomfort of being in my head for my whole life. "We had been together since we were nineteen, and so much of my identity revolved around that relationship. I wish I'd tried harder to be more independent. I think the last chance of that was when we broke up—"

Geoffrey's brow shoots up in surprise, and I realize that this is new territory. He senses my hesitation to continue and takes a step closer. We hold eye contact, and it's as if he's reached out and taken my hand. It gives me the courage to continue. "I didn't say any of this before because I didn't want it in the story. It feels too personal. And honestly, it feels a bit disloyal to talk about the low points of our marriage now that he's gone."

"I understand." He pauses and appears to be collecting his words. "Right now, I want us to both be two people interested in getting to know each other. Is that OK?"

"More than OK." A thought sneaks up on me, announcing itself so clearly that I sigh out loud: I trust this man. Fully. Not just to do right by me as a journalist but to do right by me as a person.

"We were twenty-four," I continue, "thinking about getting engaged but not quite there yet. He'd just quit his job at Google to develop OneK full time. It felt like everything became about the app, the app, the app. His mood was dependent on whether something went right or wrong with it that day. We were fighting a lot. About little things, bigger things. It was exhausting being around him, so I broke up with him."

"That couldn't have been an easy decision to make."

"It wasn't. It felt like I was walking away from the only man who'd ever love me."

"How . . . long?"

"Three months. The longest three months of my life. It was a blessing living far away from my family because I didn't have to tell anyone. I just went to work, ate, and slept a lot. Had three awful hookups that just made me miss him more. I realized I was depressed, but I couldn't bring myself to make anyone worry about me. Guess I'm still kind of like that. I'm working on it."

His eyes are filled with compassion as he leans over and runs his hand along my forearm, like he's unsure how to comfort me with so much of my skin exposed in this dress. It's a small, almost awkward gesture that fills me up.

"We ended up getting back together after bumping into each other at the grocery store, of all places. And I just slotted back into his life like nothing ever happened."

We're both quiet as chatter from the street floats up to us. A group of teens walks by, dressed for a night out. One girl struggles to keep up, her platforms too hard to walk in. A boy stops to wait for her. He bends down, and she hops on his back, yelping in the process. They move out of sight.

"You said something at volunteering that stuck with me: that I see where I fit into other people's lives."

I nod, remembering.

"It seems like you've done the same. It's easy for me to

do it with work because it's the nature of the job, and I love it. I've fallen into the habit with my friends and family, the people I already love. But I've never been able to do that with a romantic relationship."

I can see that he's tense. He runs his hand through his hair, and I want to replace it with mine.

"I've never been married—"

"Red flag for a guy over forty," I quip. "Or so I'm told." I hope my joke lands as a balm for his nerves.

Geoffrey sighs, fusses with his hair again. "I don't have much to defend myself. Just a guy who's married to his job and bad at communicating."

I frown. "How can that be true? Your whole job is about active listening and follow-up questions. I've witnessed you be good at it."

"Because I *choose* to be good at it. I actively work for it. I haven't done that in my past relationships. My last serious one ended two years ago. Her name is Annika—mutual friends set us up. At the start, it was the easiest relationship I'd ever been in."

"So, what happened?"

"I went on three back-to-back assignments, opportunities I thought were too important to pass up. I was flying back from Rome on the worst route with three layovers when I got a FaceTime call from her. Turns out, I had missed her birthday without realizing it."

I grimace. "That's pretty bad."

"Yeah, she was more resigned than upset at that point." He cringes like he doesn't want to keep going but plows ahead anyway. "Said I never considered her before I took those jobs. And she was right. She hadn't even crossed my mind."

"Seems like we've had the opposite problems in the past."

He nods. "I don't want that again. I've gone to enough therapy to know that I want to actively show up for someone I'm with. The path I've chosen is pretty lonely, and I want to see what would happen if I gave things a real shot."

"And I don't want to lose myself again."

We're dancing around the idea of us. What we want from the other. It feels too serious to directly name, but the real meaning behind our words hangs in the air between us. I know we can both see it there.

When I can't stand it anymore, I nudge him with my shoulder, and he pushes back against me. "Tell me what you're thinking right now," he says to my neck.

I lean in a little, even though we're already closer than what propriety calls for. "Are you always Geoffrey? Never Geoff?"

He laughs, soft and warm. "That's not what you're thinking right now."

I shrug, hoping I look like one of those nonchalant women from a French noir. "It's one of the things." My heartbeat picks up, and I find it hard to focus on determining what is the right thing to do now.

"What's the other?" His eyes spark, and I know he knows the answer. But he's drawing me out. Making me tell him.

My eyes drop to his mouth, and I remember the feel of

his lips pressed against mine. How good it felt, how right. "You know I can't say."

"I know you think you can't." He turns toward me so our lips are a breath apart.

My mind is racing with a hundred, a billion reasons why this is a bad idea. Thoughts of Alex, the story, the public scrutiny, his job, the foundation swim laps in my brain, but for every valid, tangible reason I should walk away, there's one reason to stay: I want to.

I want.

I want.

I want.

I haven't wanted someone like this in so long. Not even my husband, a truth I haven't let myself admit but feels obvious now. There's an ache between my thighs and a strain in my chest.

Our gazes meet, and I can tell Geoffrey sees how uncontained my desire is—how little it will take to topple me. His eyes are wild, and his breath is shallow. Our bodies crash into each other with the knowledge that there's *something* here. This time, we're not shy, not hesitant. We're searching, and each inquiry of teeth and tongues and lips is met with an answer only the other knows.

I sigh with the relief of it all, but it comes out closer to a moan. I press my breasts against his chest, creating the friction I am so desperate for. He gives me what I want, spinning me around in one fluid motion so that my back is against the wall, and he presses against me with enough pressure that I feel held but not smothered.

I forget where I am until I hear a snicker coming from the other side of the roof. I pull back, tucking my face into the side of Geoffrey's neck. A door slams.

"Do you think they recognized us?" I ask as I try to catch my breath. It's not working.

"No. I think we were too far away." His hands are warm on my back, the heat thwarting the wind.

"Do you want to go back inside?" His voice is neutral, but I know it's the last thing he wants. I feel the same way.

"No. How far is your hotel?"

"Like a fifteen-minute drive."

I shake my head. There's a chance I'd lose my courage by then, and it's been too long since I've let myself have what I want. "There's a hotel next door. Let's go there."

Geoffrey looks down at me. "Are you sure?"

I reach up, tilt his chin with my finger, and kiss him.

XIII

The ten minutes between leaving the rooftop and checking in only heighten the anticipation between us, and we barely make it into the room before I'm backing him up against the door, running my lips down his neck.

I push his jacket off his shoulders, untuck his shirt, and work as fast as I can to unbutton it. His shoulders are lightly muscled, like he works out for function, not aesthetics. I grip his biceps, enjoying the solid feel of him in my hands. It's like I'm floating, and his body is the only thing anchoring me to Earth.

His palms roam over my ass, and he cups me through the thin fabric of my dress. He kneads into me, and I feel my muscles relax with his touch. Any lingering doubt dissipated somewhere between the elevator ride and the click of the key card, and I know I'm ready to surrender completely to this.

I pull away from our kiss just enough to whisper, "Bed."

His green eyes roam my face for reassurance. I imagine my pupils are as blown as his are. I don't know how I'll feel in the morning, but for now, I am certain.

"Now," I tell him.

He spins us around, then with his lips still pressed to mine, walks me toward the bed. I feel the edge of the mattress behind my knees as Geoffrey kisses down my neck, then my shoulders, where the gown cuts away. I comb my fingers through his thick hair, and he murmurs in approval, leaning into my touch. His thumbs ghost over my nipples, but it's a tease. I'm ready to feel all of him.

I push him back gently, and confusion flickers across his face before he sees my hand move behind my back in search of my hidden zipper. I have it halfway down when the realization hits me: I haven't been naked in front of anyone new since I was twenty-four. My hand shakes, and for a second, I stop. But I scan Geoffrey's face and see nothing but warmth and a want that matches the intensity of my own.

I tug the zipper until the dress pools around my feet, and I kick it to the side. The fringe looks like confetti splayed on the floor.

Undressing myself feels important to me right now. Maybe it's because this is the first decision I'm not second-guessing. As I unpin my updo and my braids fall behind me, I feel confident. And secure. I watch the heavy rise and fall of his chest, and I hook my thumbs over the sides of my thong and step out of it.

His eyes are greedy, taking in every detail of my body, and I don't try to cover up. A month ago, I couldn't imagine being exposed like this in front of anyone. But right now, all I want is for him to see me.

"You're . . ." He swallows, as if he's trying to find the

words. "Even more than I imagined." Not more beautiful, just *more*. As if his mind can't contain all that I am. More. It's what I want for myself.

"I want to see you too." My voice is gravelly, and I like the way I sound. The way I feel. He shrugs off his shirt, and my eyes trail down to the imprint of his cock straining against his pants. He unclasps his belt buckle and pulls down his pants and underwear in one fluid motion.

I touch myself, trying to quell the growing ache that's become the center of my being.

Then he closes the distance between us, and our bodies meet, skin to skin, creating sensations I haven't felt in so long. He's careful as he pushes me back on the bed, and my body arches to meet his.

He kisses down the column of my throat, and he catches the bud of my nipple in his mouth. My body is taut as a bow as he kneads my other breast with his palm.

He moves lower, finally, to the place where I've been dying to have him. He kisses, licks, and caresses me, and I forget everything. When he presses the heel of his hand then his tongue against my clit, my mind goes blank. It's excruciating, the pleasure so heightened that it feels like pain. I don't want to come like this, not yet, and I pull him back up to me.

"Do you have a condom?"

He grins like he's about to tell me a secret, hops off the bed, and rummages through his suit jacket. I sneak a peek at the glory of his backside. Who knew a writer could look like that.

Then he's over me again. I let out a deep breath as he enters me, and he gives me a moment to adjust to the fit of him. "Good?"

I nod. When he begins to move, I let go.

I let my eyelids flutter closed and commit the feel of him to memory. The strain of the muscles in his back, the light stubble on his jaw, the soft sounds he makes when he finds the spot that makes me come undone beneath him. I squeeze my eyes tight as I unravel, like I'm trying to block out absolutely everything but the sensation of his body's effect on mine. He follows right behind me, clenching the top sheet in his fists, and when he's spent, his head falls to the crook of my shoulder. He's careful, I notice, not to put all of his weight on me. To shield me from any burden.

Once we both catch our breath, he pulls out and collapses next to me with a sigh. We're quiet, and I realize I feel playful for the first time in ages. I prop myself up on my elbow and stare down at him. His face is open and relaxed and flushed. I smooth away a lock of hair from his forehead.

"Do I get to call you Geoff now?"

He looks up at me, sleepy, with trust and a tenderness I don't want to examine. He thinks for a moment, smiles as he says, "No."

Then he pulls me down to him until I forget my own name, again and again.

XIV

I wake up slowly, after the first good night of sleep I've had since I can remember. I'm still naked, and I feel the warmth of Geoffrey behind me. Sunlight filters into the room. He gently exhales, and the hot air sends a shiver down my back. I want to stay suspended in this moment, replaying last night in my mind. The comfort of his companionship at the gala. Our conversation on the rooftop. The most intense sexual encounter I've ever had.

We woke up more than once, reaching for each other in the dark, and I learned something new each time. He likes my fingers in his mouth. He's ticklish behind his ears, but that doesn't stop him from wanting my lips there. He lets me call him Geoff when I'm on top, but I like the way the syllables of Geoffrey fall when I'm gasping for air.

I want a repeat of that feeling, of the closeness. I back into him once, twice before I feel him respond. He starts kissing my neck, and I sigh. It's too much loveliness to keep in. I twine my feet with his, and we rub against each other, lazily, in no rush, until it's obvious from the clench of my thighs that I'm ready for more. He finds another condom and eases inside me. At the start of the day instead of the end, I'm even more in tune. I feel like he's shown me the cracks in my life and makes me want to fill them.

When we finish, he wraps himself around me, and I feel the thrum of his heartbeat against my back. It's hard to think straight.

"So . . ." He traces what feels like an infinity symbol on my hip, over and over. "What do you want this to mean?"

"Why do I have to be the one to define it?" My tone is coy, but I can tell there's a crease between my brows. I'm glad he can't see it.

"Because you're the public figure. And I know what I want, but I'm not sure it's what you want."

I place my hand on top of his, lacing our fingers together. I let myself just breathe, and I'm not sure how much time passes. "I'd like to see where this goes. I haven't felt this good in a long time. Or wanted to be around someone so much."

"But?"

I laugh. "There has to be a 'but'?"

"I've been studying you." He says it with a certainty that sends a pang of guilt through me. But he hasn't seen all of me. Not yet.

"But we can't rush into anything. Not just for my sake but yours too. Your job is your everything."

"I'm starting to realize there are more important things." He traces a finger up my thigh, lays his palm flat on my stomach.

"How are you so calm about this?" I turn around to face him, and I'm pulled under by the empathy on his face. I worry he's absorbing the uncertainty I'm projecting.

"I'm not." He smooths his thumb across my forehead. "These are uncharted waters for me. I've never slept with a subject before, never had the temptation, never even gotten close. And while it's tricky, I don't think it's anything we can't work through. I'm done with your interviews, and at the end of the day, it's a profile. You're not a whistleblower; this isn't the takedown of an organization."

"You're saying I'm not that important?" I quip.

He smiles, raises his brow. "I'm saying there's some leeway. This is something we can fight for if we want to." He pulls me close. This time, I trace the infinity symbol across his ribcage. He watches me for a moment. "Is there something else?"

"I didn't think I'd be this happy again."

Geoffrey knows what I mean without me having to say it: After the accident, after Alex. He kisses my forehead. "You're allowed to be."

I want to believe him, and for this moment, I let myself.

We spend as much time as we can in the hotel room before checkout. Over room-service breakfast, we agree to keep the circle of people who know about us small: our sisters, Wendy, and Martin.

When I get home, I soak in the bath, replaying my favorite parts of the last forty-eight hours. Most are just moments of conversation between us—learning his favorites, that he was afraid of the dark until he was ten, the quiet exploration of what we want out of a relationship. I submerge myself in the pleasure of feeling close to someone new.

I throw on a robe and put on all my serums and creams when I get a FaceTime from Adamma.

"Hey, Addy—"

She cuts me off. "I haven't heard from you since Thursday, and you want to hit me with a 'Hey, Addy'?" She stops talking and looks me over. "You're glowing."

"I just got out of the bath."

"A bubble bath didn't do that to you. You had sex."

"I did." There's no point in denying it. I want her to know. Telling someone else makes it feel more real, less like a fever dream.

"With Geoffrey."

I toss back my head with a laugh. "With Geoffrey."

"How? The last time you really talked to me about him, you were freaking out about a kiss. But now you're fucking?"

"So vulgar!"

"Excuse me, you made love. You entangled souls."

"OK, OK, that's enough." She's pressing all of the little-sister buttons, like she's trying to make the elevator stop on every floor.

"How was it? Emotionally?"

I consider her question. Therapist Adamma has entered the chat. "Well. I thought it would be weird having sex with someone who wasn't Alex, but it was such a different—separate—thing. It felt natural, like that's so clearly what this was leading up to."

"That's how it should be. Do you think you'll have a repeat performance?"

"I do. But also . . ." I bite my lip. "We're going to pursue this, see where it goes. I really like being around him. He makes me laugh, makes me think about what I want. It's like my world is expanding when I'm around him."

Adamma's mouth forms a shocked "O." It's not too often I can catch her by surprise. Usually it's the other way around.

"What do you think?" When the words come out of my mouth, I realize how important her approval is to me. Just how much she's been my anchor since Alex's passing.

Adamma gives me a soft smile. "I'm happy for you."

"You don't think it's too soon?" The question ekes out of me.

"I told you before that this thing with Geoffrey could either be a one-time thing or something more. Clearly, it's something more. You owe it to yourself to explore that, fuck what anyone else might think. Hell, even me! But for the record, I just know it's good to see you looking *light* again."

I'm so light that my heart's in my throat.

XV

I look up from my computer monitor to see Wendy standing in my office door with her arms crossed over her chest and a frown. "You never told me how the gala went."

I pause my typing. "I'm glad you're feeling better. You look refreshed."

"Flattery will get you nowhere. It seems like you had a good time." She hands me a phone. The Homeless Health Care SF OneK account is on the screen, and there's a carousel of photos from the night. I'm in the first picture smiling with Oscar Gómez and his coworkers. It's fairly innocuous, and Wendy reads my confusion. "Keep scrolling."

I swipe through pictures of the other guests, and it's not until the last photo that I understand what she's referencing: We're not the main subjects of the shot, but Geoffrey and I are clear as day in the background. My hand rests on his arm, and we're both laughing. My chin is tipped up, and my eyes are closed, but he's looking right at me. There's an intimacy there someone would have to be blind not to see.

I slide the phone back to Wendy across the desk. "Yeah, it was a good night. And I got something for you in the auction. A weekend in Santa Barbara." I bring my attention back to my computer and pull up my inbox.

"Ndidi—" Her use of my first name stops me. Wendy is always formal despite my urging otherwise. I shift my attention back to her, and her expression is softer, less stern than it was before. "I'll only ask you this once: Did something happen between you and Geoffrey?"

I'm suddenly shy about telling her the truth, but I can't lie. I nod.

And Wendy does the most shocking thing I've seen her do: She throws her head back and cackles. A true belly laugh. I watch her carry on for a full minute before she collects herself. "I knew there was something there."

And that's when the penny drops. "You set me up! Were you even sick?"

Wendy shrugs. "I didn't fib about that, but maybe I exaggerated a bit. Are you mad?" Her voice is tender but serious.

I think back to the night at the hotel and the morning after. I roll my eyes and fight a grin.

"I'll take that as a no." Wendy sits down on the couch and immediately transitions into crisis-management mode. "Was last weekend the first time something happened?"

I sit up straighter. "No. We kissed a few weeks ago."

The corner of her mouth lifts in surprise, but she recovers quickly. "That's why he took a few days off."

"Right." Wendy's good at piecing small details together, one more reason why I love her.

"So, it's been ongoing since then?"

"No. We both knew it wasn't professional, so we reestablished the boundaries until he was done interviewing me. But last weekend made us realize we both want to give it a shot. And also to keep it private." I try to sum up the details in a neat package without letting my mess of feelings seep out.

"I don't need to know details, but it was more than just a kiss this time?"

"It was," I tell her, leaning forward. Wendy blushes, another first I'm witnessing. "It was more than sex though. There's something there."

Wendy raises a brow, surprised.

"It won't compromise the article if—"

"I'm not worried about the article," Wendy interjects. And now she's switched into planning mode. "My initial read is that it's more of a concern for his career than it is yours. But still, if this gets out, I wouldn't be surprised if most of the ire is directed at you. You're the woman. The widow."

I nod. There's not really much to say; a patriarchal and racist society will do what it's set up to do. "That's why we're keeping it quiet for now. We're only telling you, our sisters, and his friend Martin."

She nods, filing the information away.

"Should we ask them to take the picture down?" I ask, remembering what kicked off this conversation in the first place.

Wendy shakes her head. "I doubt there's many people looking at a nonprofit's page in the first place. The article will come out in a month, and I think it's best to slow roll your relationship. Give it a few weeks or so, then we can signal that you're seeing each other. Bury it on some loud news day."

My head is whirling. It all seems so official. I nod and sit back in my chair. "I like the sound of that."

The next two weeks move at a clip. Our work with Homeless Health Care SF and the publicity from the gala cause a flood of local organizations to reach out, and we get an influx of new proposals. Geoffrey's present throughout, coming into the office a few times a week to shadow and interview the Giga staff. We're both on our best behavior, staying away from each other in the office. But a stolen glance here and there makes me feel like I'm a teenager again. Even more so with Wendy watching us like a hawk and giving me conspiratorial looks. Like we're gushing over the cute new guy in class. All of it makes me feel carefree in a way I thought I lost.

When Geoffrey and I cuddle up on the couch in my living room after a long Thursday with my back pressed against his chest, it feels comfortable and safe. We discuss articles we've read and top off each other's glasses of wine, as if nights like this could become forever.

"Let me take you out," he whispers into my hair.

I pull away from his body to see his face. "Isn't it better to play it safe?" Since we've been seeing each other, all of our time together has been spent at my house or at Martin's bar, places where we won't run into anyone.

"I think it's a calculated risk I'm willing to take." He pulls me back against his chest, and the steady thump of his heart grounds me.

"OK, I can have Wendy book us somewhere private."

"Let me handle it. I want to actually take you out."

I frown. "Does it matter who does the booking?" I wonder if this is turning into an ego thing about who pays for what. It's not something I'd thought about before, but it hits me that most of what we've done together has been on my dime. The typical heterosexual dating dynamics have been flipped.

Geoffrey's quiet as he considers the question. "In the grand scheme of things, no, it doesn't matter. You'll always have more money than me. I'd be foolish to think that's not going to play into things, but I'm secure in what I have and what I've worked for." He squeezes my elbow. "I just want you to feel special. I want to take care of it from top to bottom." His gaze is so soft and his tone so thoughtful that I can't help myself.

"And here I thought you were about to reveal yourself as a men's rights activist," I say and kiss the ticklish spot behind his ear.

XVI

Two days later, Geoffrey has ordered us a French-Vietnamese feast at a new place called Cozette, and I'm telling him about the first and last time I took my parents on a helicopter and how my mother screamed in our headphones the entire time.

After we both stop laughing, Geoffrey cocks his head at me. "You think that kind of travel is still in your future? Helicopters, private jets, and all that?"

"I'd like to think not. I rarely do that kind of thing as it is now."

"You and Alex owned a jet for a while though?"

"Right. But we got rid of it a few years back. When he first sold the company, we were saying yes to any and every invitation, so having the jet made it easier to get around."

"I imagine." He slides the best piece of sea bass onto my plate.

"I felt so glamorous walking onto the tarmac and not having to deal with things like the TSA."

"What made you get rid of it then?"

I pause to take a bite, wanting to give the most truthful answer. "I'd like to say it was solely for the environment, but it was more the realization that we were doing all this stuff because it seemed like we were supposed to. I know that seems silly. When you have all the money in the world, no one can really make you do anything, but they sure can talk about you."

"I can understand that. There's always social pressure. It may look different, but it's always there."

I take him in in his crisp Oxford, less well worn than the ones he dresses in for his reporting. I want to know all the things he does to fit a mold. "I think I spent so much of my adult life keeping up with the Joneses—the Gateses—that I lost sight of what I actually care about." It's as much an admission as it is a revelation.

"Do you think the foundation is helping you get back to your core?"

"It is, but I still want to figure out who I am when I'm not defined by—defining *myself* by—this money."

"I get that. I've spent my whole life being so career driven. Having this one identity: Geoffrey Campbell, journalist. I want to know if there's something else out there. If there's something else *in here*." He points at his chest, and he looks me in the eye as he does. I feel the heat between us.

"I know you don't want kids, but do you ever envision yourself getting married?" I think back to one of our earlier conversations and him telling me his dad left his family early on.

Geoffrey takes a sip of wine, his brow furrowed. "Is it OK to say I still don't know? I know I'm ready for a long-term commitment, but the rest of it . . ." He trails off.

"That wasn't meant to be a trick question. Getting married again isn't something I've spent much time thinking about either. Until you, dating wasn't even something I seriously considered. I think I'm one of those people who can only focus on one area of life at a time." But when the words are out of my mouth, I wonder if they're still true. Sitting across from him in the restaurant's warm glow, I can picture another night and another and another. I can imagine us recounting our days and our work with each other. I can see the world where it all comes together, where we just keep moving.

The next evening, Geoffrey leaves town for a string of interviews, and after I finish going over a grant package with Elijah, I take the elevator downstairs to meet Bill. I'm thinking about slipping my heels off and having a nice glass of wine when I spot Henry in the lobby. He has no reason to be here. There's nothing scheduled with the board. I hold my breath, knowing whatever's coming can't be good.

Henry spots me. "Didi! Just thc person I wanted to see. I was hoping to catch you."

I plaster on a smile. "Yeah, I was on my way home. It's been a long week."

"I bet. You have time for a quick chat? Maybe a drink?"

"Ah, I have plans to get to," I lie through my teeth.

"I promise it won't take too long. How about we walk around the block?"

Hard to get out of that. "All right." I shrug and text Bill. Henry and I join a stream of commuters, and I have to put in a little effort to keep up with him.

"I won't beat around the bush: I saw you and Campbell out last night."

I want to stop walking, but I know a measured response is the best one right now. "You did?"

"At Cozette. I was going to stop by and say hello, but you two looked pretty cozy. Didn't want to interrupt."

"It's unlike you to not make your presence known." It's petty, but I can't miss the opportunity.

He laughs, but there's no warmth in it. "Do you really think getting involved with Campbell is a good idea?" The faux sheen of sincerity in his tone makes me stop in my tracks, forcing Henry to do the same.

"Look, Henry, I think you're overstepping—"

"C'mon, Didi, don't bullshit me. I see the way you look at each other. It was obvious at the gala and even more so last night."

I know it wouldn't be wise to admit to anything, but I can't bring myself to outright deny what he saw either. "Why do you care so much?"

"I'm just looking out for you." He says it matter-of-factly and throws up his hands. As though the two of us having this conversation—this argument—in the middle of the sidewalk is remotely appropriate.

"I didn't ask you to," I say, keeping my voice controlled.

"You didn't, but if your impropriety gets out, how do

you think that will make Giga look? I just want you to think about it."

"I think as long as we're doing good work, it won't matter." My answer sounds Pollyanna–ish even to my own ears. But I want it to be true. Need it to be true.

Henry shrugs. "In a perfect world. I know we haven't always been the closest, but . . . Alex was one of my best friends. It haunts me that he was on his way to see me when he died." His voice falters, and I think it's the first honest thing I've heard him say in a year.

"It was an accident," I say softly. I step under an awning, and he follows me. I'm hoping I can shift the tone here.

"I know." He shakes his head, and it's like he flips a switch. All of his vulnerability dissipates. "I'm sure Alex would want you to move on eventually, but this guy? He's a journalist. You can't trust the press. Thought we all knew that by now."

"You don't know him."

Henry holds up his hands in defense. "I'm not sure you do either. I'm not the bad guy here. Think about what I'm saying."

"I don't need to. Just leave this alone, Henry. Please."

He narrows his eyes but doesn't say anything. I reach for my phone and ask Bill to pull around. When he walks off with nothing but a dip of his chin, I exhale, out and in, out and in.

But it doesn't help. I'm fuming. Henry's brought me back to feeling like that scared twenty-three-year-old version of myself who didn't know how to stand up for herself. Part of me knows that it's no one's business what's going on between Geoffrey and me, but I don't want this to become the kind of scandal that blows back on Giga. It's my money we're giving away, but there's still a team of people I have to consider. And there's also Geoffrey's career to protect. It all feels so convoluted; I can't think straight. "Fuck, fuck, fuck," I mutter to myself when I realize I don't know what to do anymore.

XVII

I send Geoffrey a text that night recounting Henry's confrontation knowing that he's on a flight for a reporting trip and it may be a while before he sees it. I call Wendy, annoyed we're both doing this with our Friday nights, and we agree there's not much to do about it. If Henry opts to make it a problem, we'll respond. It's an unsatisfactory solution, but it's the one we have for the time being. I spend Saturday puttering around the house, swimming, and watching an old season of *Love Island.* Hot dummies falling in love are an excellent distraction, and I'm thankful for them.

Geoffrey messages to see how I'm faring and to confirm that he's back on Sunday, and I decide to surprise him at the Airbnb he's booked for this stint. Chef Aaron packs us pasta and picks out a nice bottle of wine for me to bring.

When Geoffrey opens the door, he's in gray sweatpants, a hoodie, and a pair of black Clark Kent glasses. His hair is slightly damp, and his feet are bare. It's clear he's fresh out of the shower. He looks a little tired, and even so, he's the best thing I've seen.

"Hey! What're you—" I catch the surprise on his face before he tucks it away.

I hold up the provisions. "I missed you."

His eyes soften, and if I didn't already think I was falling in love with him, I wouldn't have a shred of plausible deniability now.

"Thank you." He pulls me into him, and when he kisses me, it isn't with the heat I'm expecting after days away from each other. It's more tender, truer. Geoffrey leads me inside and plates the food, and we sit down to eat at the kitchen table. I don't want to jump into the Henry drama; instead, I ask him how the trip was.

He clears his throat. "Right. So, you know I've been wrapping up the profile, and I had a few more interviews to do for background." He stops, seems hesitant. Uncertainty isn't a look I'm used to seeing on him. I nod, urging him to get on with it.

"I spoke with Danny Oliveira." Alex's cofounder. "He was hard to find, but through some surf groups, I was able to figure out he's actually in California. Cortes Bank, near San Diego."

My palms begin to sweat, and my already chaotic heartbeat goes into overdrive. I know where this is going, and this is my final chance to say it to him before he says it to me. "Danny told you I coded OneK, didn't he?" I spit out the words, and the shock of them leaving my mouth makes my hands shake.

Geoffrey nods. "He did."

"Why?" I have so many questions, but this is the first. After all this time, I didn't expect him to say anything.

"He thought now that Alex is gone, you were willing to tell the truth. He figured that was what the profile was about. I didn't get the sense he was trying to out your secret or anything."

I rest my hands on the table, trying to still them and taking it all in. "Danny's not the kind of guy to talk to journalists."

"What do you mean?" Geoffrey's features are inscrutable, and I wonder how much he's turned this new information about me over in his head.

"It took a lot of convincing on both Alex's and my part to get him to agree to it. It never sat right with him. So after your piece on Alex and the company back then, Danny bowed out of doing press. He left it to Alex."

Geoffrey looks down, almost guilty.

Then I see it. "Have you been suspicious about this the whole time?"

"I have been. When I interviewed Alex, he did this thing where he said 'we' when he talked about coming up with the app. He only let it slip a time or two, and I didn't think much of it at first. I assumed he was confusing his timeline, talking about Danny. But then there were the things he said about you. 'Ndidi's the smartest person I've ever met' and 'She's going to change the world someday; she's already changed mine.'"

"That wasn't in the piece." I've read it enough times to know.

"No, I figured he was just a guy in love. But his words popped back into my head when I met you. So I did what I should have done years ago and outright asked Danny about your involvement. He told me Alex confided in him about using code based on your work."

I sigh, feeling the weight of it all release with my breath. I knew it would feel bad if this information ever got out but didn't imagine I might experience other, more complicated emotions too. "We conceptualized it together, and I did the initial coding for it. But Alex was the one to take it from a prototype to something real. I backed away from the project pretty early on."

"But why? That's my real question here." He leans forward, and I'm brought back to our first meeting when he did the same thing, like he was on the edge of his seat for my answer. Like he cared what it was.

"Why does it matter? I don't want to dwell. I just care about the foundation and moving forward."

"Because it's a part of you, a part of your story."

"Is this just about the profile?" I can't help but ask.

"God, no. Ndidi. I want to know why you'd do something like that. As a person, not as a subject. Why would you back away from something like that, something that presumably meant so much to you?" His voice cracks in frustration.

I pick up my napkin, twist it. Geoffrey's eyes dart to my hands, and I feel like I'm on display. I stop, place my hands on my lap instead. Rub them along the fabric of my pants. "I told you about my first job out of school. It was awful and made me realize that wasn't a world I wanted to be a part of."

"Wouldn't this have been different? The two of you starting something together from the ground floor? You could have created a different kind of work environment."

"In an ideal world, sure. But that's not the world we're living in. Not now and especially not then." I let out a low laugh, one laced with resentment. "I'd lost my appetite for being the only woman in the room, one of the only people of color. And it wasn't just the office. When you're looking for investors, it's easier for them to give you money if you look like them. If they feel like you're the right kind of person."

"A white guy," he supplies.

I arch my brows. "I didn't want to get in the way of Alex succeeding."

"I don't understand how you think Alex's success was more important than your own. Or how he let you do that."

I'm silent for a long time. Trying to formulate the perfect response when I know there isn't one. "He was just trying to support me. At the time, I was so rattled and confused. My dad was sick. Hell, I was sick. Had a stress ulcer after that job. But Alex was the opposite. He absolutely came alive when it came to doing the kind of work that just filled me with dread."

"You were never jealous about it? Close enough to know what was going on but not a part of the team?" He asks with a bit of incredulity in his voice.

"In the beginning, I was. Because tech was the thing I

was supposed to be doing but couldn't. Or didn't believe I could. But as the company took off, I felt more disconnected from it. Sure, it started with me, but it didn't grow with me."

"What about the money? I know it was impossible to know what it would become at the time. But I'm sure there was the dream of building a successful business? Of exiting?"

I sigh, embarrassed to think about how naive I was. "At the start, there wasn't any money. And he was the one who put in the initial investment from his grandparents to build it out. We were married by the time the app was monetized, so I got shares in the company. If things had worked out differently and we'd never gotten married, then I would have fought for my credit. But that didn't happen."

It's a thought I've had many times over the years, wondering what would have become of me if I'd been forced to figure out my career. Would I have tried another start-up, or would I have left San Francisco for good? Gone back to school and done something to satisfy my parents? I'll never know.

"And at the root of it all, I enjoyed having the money!" I haven't let myself express that aloud to anyone, and I say it louder and more emphatically than I mean to. "I was in a situation I created, so it was easier to just ignore the bad feelings about how it all played out. It wasn't until Alex died that I stepped back and realized how hollow it all felt."

Geoffrey's brow furrows like he's still trying to wrap his mind around my reasoning. "What about now that you're getting rid of it all? Don't you think it's time people knew the truth?"

"I care more about what I can use the money for and the good I can do with it. That's something I have in my control now."

He runs a hand through his hair. A few days ago, I might have smoothed it, but now I can't tell if that's appropriate. He sighs, and there's exasperation there. "I'm having a hard time figuring out why you agreed to this profile then."

I shrug. "Some misguided outcry of my ego? Hubris, thinking I hid it so long ago that it wouldn't come up?"

"Don't be glib." There's no heat to his words, but there is a hint of building frustration.

"I really don't know how else to be right now. I just know I don't want to ruin Alex's legacy. Turn him into that guy who stole from his wife, because that's not what this is."

"Are you sure?" Geoffrey crosses his arms over his chest. Is he being protective of a past version of me?

"I'm sure. It was one of the only things Alex and I fought about. He wanted to include me as a cofounder, but every time he brought it up, I shut the conversation down."

I stop talking. A flashback to one of our biggest fights replays in my mind. Geoffrey watches me closely, and I can feel him trying to decipher every microexpression. "It was the reason we broke up briefly. As much as he loved me, I think this was the one thing he couldn't understand about me."

"It's every bit your legacy as it is his. You could go on the record and say everything you just told me." There's a fire forming in his eyes, an idea taking shape.

I shake my head. "I just . . . I don't know. I need to think about this."

He leans back and lets out a sigh. "I don't know why you won't let me—" But he stops, correcting himself. I realize I'm holding my breath, knowing what he was about to say but feeling scared to hear it. "I don't know why you won't let the world in. You're brilliant. You're as kind as you are frustrating."

"I've been told," I say, trying to find the humor in the situation when I feel none.

He interlaces his fingers in front of his chest. "I just wish you could see yourself from my perspective. See the woman I'm falling—"

I cut him off. "Please, don't go there." It's too much for my nervous system to take.

Geoffrey flinches like I hit him. And in a way, I suppose I have. But he must see the same hurt reflected on my face because he just nods, lips pursed like he's actively holding his thoughts in.

"Are you putting this in the piece?" I ask, just as Geoffrey says, "So where does this leave us?"

I wait for him to go first. "I don't know."

"I need some time to think through things," I tell him. "Can you give me that?"

"I will," he says, and we lean into each other at the same time. The kiss is bittersweet, salty from the tears I only now realize have started to fall down my cheeks.

XVIII

I wake up the next morning in my own bed with a pounding headache, as if I'd been drinking all night. The reality is much lamer: I cried myself to sleep. Cried for the past catching up to me, cried at the way that this reveal could put both my and Alex's legacy under a microscope, cried for the new uncertainty between Geoffrey and me—just when I was starting to get comfortable with the idea of there being a Geoffrey and me.

I take a shower and throw on a knit dress I'm 90 percent sure I wore on Friday. I can't bring myself to care. I see a missed call from Adamma, but I ignore that too.

I make it to the office by nine and seek out Wendy, who's already at her desk furiously typing emails. Part of me wants to go over to her and tell her that Geoffrey knows about OneK, but I don't feel ready.

She looks up at me. "How was the rest of your weekend?"

"It was OK."

"Just OK?" She looks around before whispering, "I thought Geoffrey came back?"

"He did, but he was really tired, so I only got to see him

briefly." The lie rolls off my tongue. I walk into my office and close the door behind me to avoid further conversation.

I try to look over a proposal package Elijah's flagged, but my inbox dings. An email from Geoffrey.

Ndidi—

I know we left things a bit weird last night. I couldn't sleep, so I did what I knew how to do and wrote. I'm proud of this piece. I think it's one of the best things I've written. I took our conversation into account, and I did my best to tell the truth while honoring things you want to keep private. It was a tricky balance, but I think I got it right. If you're uncomfortable with it, I won't publish it. I never thought I'd get to the place where a relationship was more important than my work, but the time I've spent with you is. Call me greedy, but I want more. Let me know by next Monday what you want me to do.

Yours,

G

I hover my cursor over the attachment. A minute goes by. Another one. I don't know how long I end up sitting there, afraid to see what he's written about me. Which is stupid because I trust him, and I know anything Geoffrey writes is deeply considered. And yet, I can't bring myself to read it.

There's a knock on my door that stirs me out of my trance. "Come in." I minimize the email as if I were caught watching porn.

Wendy pops her head in. "Simone and I are going to make a Philz run, you want anything?"

"No, thanks."

Wendy crosses her arms over her chest. "OK, what's going on? You came in looking glum, you've been holed up in your office, and now you're refusing Philz. Don't lie to me."

Suddenly, my morning headache comes back in full force. I massage my temple. "I don't want to get into it, but I lied about seeing Geoffrey. I went over to his place, and let's just say we had a tough conversation."

Wendy uncrosses her arms and takes a seat in front of my desk. "Your first one?"

I nod.

"Was it something petty?"

"No."

"A deal-breaker?"

"Honestly, maybe." I don't want to ask him to compromise his journalistic integrity, but I'm not sure I'm ready to blow up my own life in the process.

Wendy lets out a low whistle. "I wasn't expecting that. But I think you have to ask yourself if you want to make it work. You'd be surprised what solutions you can come to if you're committed. Without that, there's no point."

I press my palm against my forehead like I'm testing for a fever. She's right. I just need to figure out if I'm committed. Simple.

She gets up to leave. Pats my hand. "So, how do you want to handle the rest of today?"

"Drown myself in Giga. Give out $20 million this week?"

She smiles. "We can do that."

By Wednesday, we've allotted $10 million across organizations that advance women's health care and protect abortion rights. And though throwing myself into work is effective during the day, I find myself dreading the evening hours. Going home alone. Eating alone. In the house I used to share with my dead husband. I find myself staring at my phone, willing Geoffrey's name to pop up on the screen. He's reached out to me every day for general check-ins, but I find myself giving the bare minimum in reply. It's hard when there's so much I want to say, but I don't have access to the language to say it. Not right now. It's clear he's leaving the ball in my court.

He calls me on Thursday. I'm in the middle of getting ready when I see his contact picture light up on my phone screen, a candid I snapped of him at Martin's, laughing at some years-old joke between the two of them. My fingers itch to pick up the call, but I restrain myself. I don't want him to ask me if I've read the profile yet. I let it go to voicemail, and I immediately listen to his message.

"Ndidi. I didn't expect you to answer, but I hoped you would. I know you need some time to sort things out. I get that. I'm not trying to pressure you. I just want to hear your voice." He sounds unsure of himself in a way that makes my stomach tighten, and I know that it's because of me.

I hear him clear his throat, and my stomach clenches.

Nothing good can come from this shift. "Also, I should mention, I'm leaving San Francisco soon. My editor wants me to go to South Dakota for that story. I don't know when I'll be able to come back. If you even want that. Just let me hear from you, OK? I better go before this thing cuts me off." The message ends, and I sink down on my bed. I want to call him back, but I still don't have any answers. Not about the article, our relationship, any of it.

There's only one person I can process all my thoughts with. I pick up the phone and make a call. "Can I come see you?"

I land in Richmond by 6 p.m. and take a car to Adamma's. I only told her I was coming this morning, but Adamma's not one to be fazed by the world's shortest notice. She started making up the guest room as we spoke. Elijah and Wendy both assured me they'd hold down the fort without asking for any explanation.

It's been such a long time since I've been back here. It doesn't feel like any kind of home anymore. But it's a place where I have roots, and that's grounding. On the drive, I scan the side of the highway for everything that's changed and what's stayed the same. I barely have a chance to get out of the car when Adamma runs out of the house and crushes me against her. I'm not the most tactile person, but there's something about being held by her—by someone who loves me. I can feel her pour all her care and compassion into me, and it hits me how few times I've let her do this. I realize I'm crying and pull back to wipe away my tears.

"What's going on?" Adamma's voice is full of concern.

"I'm just . . . it's been a lot." I don't even know where to start. My entire life is different than it was a year and a half ago in every way that matters?

"You can tell me all about it later," she says, and as soon as we're inside, Jalen comes barreling into me. Like mother, like son.

"Auntie Didi, look!" he screams and jumps into my arms, shoving a crumpled piece of paper in my face. "I made it for you." It's a card with a stick-figure woman, a sad face, and a broken heart. It says, "Be happy."

"Thank you, I love it." But I look at Adamma, the question clear in my eyes.

She shrugs. "He could tell I was worried about you."

Tyrique walks in and gives me a side hug on the way to the fridge. "Good to see you, Didi." I like Tyrique. He's a poet and a professor, and yet he's the one person I can gang up on Adamma with when she gets into her holier-than-thou mode. He also had a special relationship with Alex, more than anyone else in my family. They'd go golfing together on our family vacations, spending hours on the course talking about I have no idea what. "Don't disappear on us again, OK?"

"I won't," I say through the lump in my throat, absorbing how much my avoidance affects the people who love me. And it's exactly what I'm doing to Geoffrey right now.

"Wash up; we're about to eat," Adamma calls out over

her shoulder. When I step into the bathroom, I wash my hands and look in the mirror. I definitely don't appear light now. There are hollows where no one wants to have hollows.

I roll my eyes at myself. Enough is enough. I pull out my phone and text Geoffrey, and I don't let myself belabor the message. I write it once, straight through, and hit send.

Ndidi: Hi, I'm sorry I missed your call. And that I've been nonresponsive. It's shitty of me. I just need more time to process. I left SF this morning. I'm in Virginia with Adamma. I miss you.

To my surprise, he writes back almost immediately.

Geoffrey: I'm glad you're with your family. Thanks for letting me know what's going on. I'm here if you need to talk.

Ndidi: I know. Thank you.

Before I can catch my breath, he sends me a video of prairie dogs going in and out of their holes at a frenetic pace that makes me laugh.

Geoffrey: Where today's reporting has led me.

I grin down at my dumb screen. My God, he gives me more grace than I deserve. I put my phone away and manage not to think about it all through dinner. Afterward, Jalen gives me a tour of his Bluey stuffed animals and, despite my shitty voices, makes me read him the same book four times in a row. I almost cry when I see *Julián Is a Mermaid* on his shelf.

After Jalen has gone to sleep, Tyrique makes a half-hearted excuse to give Adamma and me alone time. The two of us change into our pajamas, grab popcorn and wine, and snuggle up on the couch with our heads resting on opposite ends and a shared blanket draped over our legs like we did when we were kids. We both know it's time for me to tell her why I'm here.

"OK, really. What's going on?" Adamma asks. She keeps her expression neutral, but I know how hard it is for her to hide the concern in her eyes.

I want to grab a throw pillow, to fidget with the tassels and avoid eye contact, but I force myself to look at her directly. "What if I told you I've been lying about something to you, to everyone, for the past fourteen years?"

Her face twists in confusion. "About what?"

"About OneK." My heart races fast enough to rival a hummingbird's. I'm not scared of Adamma not believing me, but I am scared of what it means to speak a truth I've been so scared to say. Of what it means to out myself as someone who deceives everyone the way I have. What it means to be a liar. I take a deep breath and hold it. I exhale out my words. "I was the one who wrote the initial code that started the whole thing."

"You're joking." She looks me over, scanning for any indication this is some elaborate ruse. When she finds none, her face falls. "Why are you telling me this now?"

"Geoffrey figured it out through writing the profile. He spoke to Danny, the only other person who knows."

"Didi, what? How could we—how could *I*—not know that?" I can tell she's running back through memories, looking for signs she missed.

"I didn't *want* you to know it. I didn't want anyone to. Hell, not even me."

"But why? Did Alex . . ." She trails off.

I shake my head and pull the blanket higher over my chest. "No, I was the one who made him keep it a secret. My head was so fucked up after my first job out of school. I doubted myself, was so embarrassed I couldn't tough it out. I was worried I wasn't as strong as we were raised to be." My breath shudders, and I do everything I can to keep my tears at bay. I know I could cry, but I want this to be about Adamma and not me. "I didn't have the heart to defend myself or the strength to fight back against the boys' club and the racism, so in my mind it became easier to remove myself from the whole world."

Adamma chews her bottom lip, a childhood habit that signals distress. I hate that I'm the one who's making her feel this way. After a moment, she presses her fingertips to her mouth to stop the tick. "I can understand not wanting to stay in a hostile environment. I don't fault you for that. But I am having a hard time understanding why you felt like you couldn't come to me. At any point in time." Her voice cracks, and my heart twists. I'm supposed to be the big sister here, someone who protects her from pain, not causes it.

"I was scared. It grew so quickly, and then it was impossible to backpedal. I rationalized it to myself every day in the beginning, and then I just tried to put it out of my mind. I told myself that at the end of the day, it didn't matter because I loved Alex, and it was our life together, our money. And I think the deeper thing is, I was ashamed. I didn't want anyone, especially not you, to think less of me. For selling myself short. For not pushing through." I shift forward and reach for her fingers, and I flash back to us as children, holding hands when we were scared of the dark. Then my tears fall. Adamma grips my hand tighter, and I squeeze back. I look at her, and she's crying too. Neither of us is attempting to stop.

"This is a lot to process. I want to tell you I'm not mad at you, but I am. But more than that, I hurt for you and the fact that you had to shoulder this on your own all this time."

"Please don't feel that way."

"You'd think by now you'd know you can't rationalize your emotions away." She says it through tears but with a smile, in her slightly bossy therapist tone, and I know we'll be OK. "I want you to know you don't have to hide from the people you love," she says. "Me, our parents, who will definitely have a field day with this—"

"God, I don't want to think about that conversation yet."

"I'll be there when you tell them if you want me to." She squeezes my hand. "And what about Geoffrey?"

I look up at the ceiling, preparing to unveil more of my avoidant bullshit. "He sent me the article. I haven't read it yet."

"Why not?"

"Because I don't have the answers yet. How it affects Giga, the uproar it could cause . . . Honestly though, I'm just not sure I'm ready to see myself through Geoffrey's eyes."

"I think the first two concerns are things you'll figure out in time. But if Geoffrey's someone important to you . . ."

"I mean, I don't know exactly what my future looks like, but I know I want him with me."

"Then let him see you. Revealing our true selves is a gift we can give each other, and that reciprocity of being received for who we are—it's a major gift. The biggest. I know the courage it takes to let someone love you, but you have that. Don't forget it."

Adamma hugs me and points to the clock. It's nearly midnight. She takes herself to bed, but I stay on the couch, playing back everything she just said. I take out my phone and pull up the article.

He opens by describing my journey from self-imposed exile in London to equally self-imposed return to California to start Giga Giving. He takes time explaining the ins and outs of a limited-life foundation, how our ten-year lifespan gives the project a unique urgency and momentum. Wendy, Elijah, and Simone make appearances in the piece, framed as my "secret weapons." He gets quotes from Janet Young and Oscar Gómez about how they're already using the grant money to change their organizations.

He writes about Alex: how much I still love him and how much Alex said he learned from me during their previous interview. Geoffrey reflects that he wishes he'd had a chance to talk to me back then. I read those lines two, then three times, overwhelmed to see that truth in print. He quotes Danny on the record saying, "There'd be no OneK without Ndidi Davis. I'm glad she's making her mark on the world now." The whole paragraph gracefully toes the line of a revelation without explicitly saying it.

Geoffrey recounts my professional exit from Silicon Valley, conveys how rudderless I'd felt despite having all the money in the world. And how it appears, from his perspective, as if I've found my purpose. The last line of the piece quotes Alex: "Ndidi's going to change the world someday; she's already changed mine."

Geoffrey's writing style is descriptive without being florid, and the picture he paints invites the reader into my life. It invites *me* to see my life from a bird's-eye view—maybe more accurately than I can from up close. When I'm done reading, I'm bowled over. I can't believe what Geoffrey is reflecting back to me in this piece. And that I've pushed him away. A man who honors the relationship I had with Alex and makes me feel like a new love is possible, one without any secrets or shame. A man who encourages me to grow into the person I'm trying to be. I go to bed knowing that I have to fight for him. But that I have to fight for myself first.

XIX

I spend the rest of the weekend in Richmond playing with Jalen and cooking dinner with Adamma. The whole time with Geoffrey's words on a loop in my head. We get our parents on FaceTime, and I tell both them and Tyrique about OneK. There are tears, confused expressions, and a lot of questions, but like with Adamma, I feel their love more than anything else.

On Monday morning, I take the first flight back to San Francisco and call Wendy when I land at 6 a.m., feeling a bit guilty but knowing she'll be up.

"Ndidi, is something wrong?"

I smirk that she's used my first name for the second time. Feel like it's becoming the new norm. "Yes, and no. We need to call an emergency board meeting. There are a few things I need to come clean about, and I want them to hear it directly from me."

Wendy's silent, but I feel like I can hear her thinking. "Should I be concerned?"

"Not anymore," I say with a confidence I didn't realize I've been lacking. "I'm going to forward you an email with the draft of Geoffrey's profile attached. I want it to go to everyone."

"OK, consider it done. I'll get the meeting on the books."

"Thank you. For trusting me. For everything really."

"There's no need."

I arrive for the meeting power-dressed in heels and a suit that feels as close to protective armor as I'm going to get. When I get to the office, half of the board members are here in person and half are on Zoom, projected on the big screen. When I walk into the conference room, everyone stops talking. I step in front of the empty seat between Wendy and Elijah, who both give me nods of encouragement, but I don't sit down. I brush imaginary lint off my jacket and stand up a little straighter before I address the room.

"Thank you all for being here today. I know I've caused a bit of alarm. Safe to assume everyone's read Geoffrey's article?" I'm met with general murmurs of agreement.

"I have a question," Henry says. "What the hell did I just read?" Before I can respond, he continues. "Campbell just barely skirted making some pretty big claims, and without Alex around to defend himself. It's not like Didi created OneK. You're going to let him publish this?" Henry looks to Wendy, as if I'm not even in the room.

Wendy turns to me like, *Should I take this?* but I shake my head. "There's nothing to make a statement about. Everything Geoffrey alluded to is true." I keep my voice steady and assertive. Once I say it, I know I can't take it back, so I want to be clear. "Alex had the initial idea, but it was something we conceptualized together. And I was the one who wrote the first codebase." I feel my shoulders drop an inch.

Henry shakes his head. "Come *on*, you just can't go around saying that."

"I can. I just did."

"But it's not the truth. I was close with Alex. He would have told me."

"No, he wouldn't have. Alex was my husband, Henry. And I didn't want anyone to know. Until now, Danny Oliveira was the only person aware. He's the one who told Geoffrey."

Henry's mouth is open, but Nicole cuts in. "When is the article coming out?"

"The end of the week." *After I give Geoffrey the go-ahead*, I don't say.

"Am I the only one living in reality here?" Henry interjects. "This looks terrible. Your little boyfriend can't publish this."

"What are you talking about?" Elijah's eyes dart back and forth between us, visibly thrown by this left turn. I should have known Henry would resort to this.

"That's the second thing I wanted to talk about today. I'm seeing Geoffrey. Romantically." The second bomb goes off, but after the OneK reveal, the response is somewhat muted. "We tried to approach the situation as ethically as possible. I understand the optics don't look great, but my relationship with him is private. It's not up for debate. Just know that he wasn't working on my behalf. I didn't want any of this to come out initially, but now that it has, I don't regret it."

"This is ridiculous, Didi—"

"It's Ndidi." I focus on my breathing, keeping my voice steady. "Henry, why do you even want to be here? I don't know if it's your grief over Alex or your misplaced sense of duty to protect his legacy, but that's my job, not yours. And I sure as hell didn't ask for your input on my personal life." I finally take my seat. "I think it's in the foundation's best interest if you resign from the board."

Henry's mouth gapes open and closed, like a fish gasping for air. He looks around the room for support, but when he finds none, he stands up. "Fine. Consider this my informal resignation."

"Received. Thank you. Wendy and our lawyers will follow up with the paperwork."

Henry grabs his bag and leaves.

The room is silent. Everyone looks to me. "If any of you feel differently about working with me given the information I've shared, I respect if you decide to resign."

The temperature in the room is hard to read at first. But after an hour of conversation and questions about my rationale for concealing my involvement with OneK, the general consensus is that while it's not ideal optics-wise, it ultimately won't affect the work we're doing with our charity partners. No one else resigns, and I leave the office to meet Bill with the car. I press my forehead against the wall of the elevator, relieved and thankful that didn't blow up in my face.

I FaceTime Adamma from the backseat. "I got Henry to resign!" My voice is louder and more fiery than I expect.

"Finally!" she shouts back. "Girl, that guy was bad news from day one. You always hated him."

Bill looks at me through the rearview mirror. "Oh yeah, even I knew that."

They've got me there. "I just thought, after everything... And Alex trusted him."

"But I'm sure he didn't talk down to Alex at every opportunity like he did with you," Adamma says.

Bill murmurs along in agreement, and given the way he usually holds his tongue, it's clear nobody around me is going to mourn Henry's departure. That everyone around me could see the situation more clearly than I did. A pattern, it seems.

After I tell Adamma the whole story, she puts on her most gentle voice. "How do you feel?"

"I think I feel good. I mean, I *do* feel good." I self-correct before she can therapize me. "And also—I haven't spoken to Geoffrey through all of this. But I'm ready now."

XX

When I call Wendy to see if she can figure out Geoffrey's South Dakota schedule, she laughs, that same guffaw she revealed after the gala. "I was waiting for you to ask for my help. Of course I can."

There are no direct flights going to Rapid City, South Dakota, so Wendy charters a private jet. The rational part of my brain knows I could have simply called him, but I don't want to have this conversation on the phone. And what's the point of having all this money if I can't throw it around every now and then, when it really matters?

I land a little past 8 p.m. and rent a Dodge Charger, one of the only cars on the lot. After some trial and error, I'm on the road, preparing to ambush him at a diner. Wendy, who is relishing this assignment with the zest of a plucky PI, got the tip-off from the motel clerk that he's eaten there every night since he's been in town. The highway is dark and quiet, but there's something calming about how deserted it is. I pull into the parking lot in the sleepy downtown and kill the engine. Check my reflection. Not light exactly, but not as heavy. When I walk in, the diner is empty save for a few people at the counter and a lone man with his back to me in a booth. His hair is a little grown out and brushes the back of his denim chore coat. I smile at getting to witness him from this perspective.

"Take a seat anywhere; I'll get to you in a sec," the man behind the counter tells me, but I'm already halfway to Geoffrey's table. As I slide into the seat across from him, he looks up from the menu, and I watch, with a bit of unconcealed glee, as his eyes widen in surprise.

"I—You—What? What're you doing here?"

"Making a gesture that would be totally creepy if it wasn't coming from the right person," I say. On the flight, I racked my brain for something witty and romantic to say. Then it dawned on me that I should channel the confidence that had been nascent in me for so long. That is now coming back full force. "I just hope I'm that right person for you." I try to keep my tone light despite knowing the stakes. My left foot is tapping, and my heart is hammering out of my chest. Geoffrey leans back, thinking, but doesn't say anything.

"I told my family and the board about my role in OneK," I say.

He exhales. "How did that go?"

"Surprisingly? It went OK. My family was hurt I'd waited so long. I should have trusted that they love me enough to know the truth. Their reaction made me realize that I don't want to hide anymore. I sent the board your article, and I asked Henry to resign."

He arches that right eyebrow. "Guessing he didn't take the news well?"

"Correct. He tried to use my relationship with you against me." I notice Geoffrey flex his hand on the tabletop. "I didn't let him. I don't care who knows about us. I want you to publish the article. I'm sorry it took me so long to read it, Geoffrey. The way you write, God, it—it showed me a version of myself I thought I'd lost, one where I'm capable of so much more than I thought."

He shakes his head. "I didn't write some idealized version of who you are, Ndidi. I just described who I see."

"This is why I love you." The words tumble out, but I'm not done. "I'm ready to weather whatever comes with putting the story out there. I don't care anymore at this point, as long as I get to be with you."

His face goes soft. He parts his lips, but he doesn't say anything. I know he's turning over his words in his head. He gave me space, so I sit with my unease.

"Ndidi, I barely heard from you all week." He's clearly hurt, and I know he has every right to be.

"I'm sorry. I needed time. I needed to fix everything first."

"I get that, but I wanted to be there for you, to help you through it. Not to pressure you but to just be. You shut me out, and that scares me. Because I love you too."

I've known this on a visceral level for weeks now, but my breath still catches, hearing it from him. "It took a lot for me to write the article the way I did. Usually, I write without compromise, but this time, when it came to you, I wanted to compromise. I wanted to put you first because that means there's an us, and that's the only thing I want right now." He says it with so much conviction that I feel the force of his words reverberate through my body.

"Us is all I want. I needed to close the door on OneK and the shit I've carried for way too long. I can't promise I won't try to shut you out when my emotions are high, old habits die hard and all that, but I promise I will work on it. You've shown me that there's a different way to be, that I don't have to live in such a burdened way anymore. I want a future with you. If you'll have me."

His hand is on the table, resting by his menu. I place mine over it, and the action grounds me like I knew it would. I feel a tear prick at the corner of my eye and wipe it away with my free hand.

He flips his palm over, intertwining our fingers. "I'd like that too." He leans over the table, and I meet him halfway. We kiss, and it feels like a deep sigh of relief, like being in a soaking tub, fully at ease.

Geoffrey takes me back to his motel, a far cry from the hotel we stayed in the night of the gala. We undress each other slowly, like we have all the time in the world because now, we know it'll stick. I linger with each kiss, I comb my fingers through his hair, and I keep my eyes on his when he's inside me. I'm trying to tell him everything I said at the diner but this time with my body.

I whisper, "I'm here, I'm here, I'm here," until it becomes a refrain. I hold him close, my arms around his neck as we finish, and he breathes into the spot behind my ear that, admittedly, is a little ticklish for me too.

We don't talk about all of the things that lie ahead of us: navigating the inevitable backlash to his story, to our relationship. What any of this means for our work, our schedules, our lives. We both know we'll figure it out, and none of that matters right now.

I want us, I want us, I want us.

And now I get to have us.

For a look into Ndidi and Geoffrey's future together and how the foundation ends, read the epilogue and dive into the whole world of this anti-billionaire billionaire romance. Just scan below or visit 831stories.com/majorgift.

More novellas like this one are waiting for you at 831stories.com, where we celebrate romantic fiction in all its forms. You can also dive into bonus content, products, events, and fan fiction and join our membership program to receive new releases early, get discounts across the site, and access all sorts of exclusive perks.

ACKNOWLEDGMENTS

Many thanks to my parents, Peter and Faye. Your unwavering faith in me allows me to pursue this madness of a career path, and I'm eternally grateful for you. And to Debbie, I miss you and know you're watching over me.

Thank you to Brittani, PJ, and Lisa, my Adammas who give me reality checks and sage advice and make me laugh the most.

Thank you to Brittain and Maddy, my BBs! Both of you were my sounding boards for my random plot questions, styling consultations, and procrastination freak-outs. Happy to return the favor, forever and always.

To my LA (spiritually, if not physically anymore) friends who keep me going: Selam, Jen, Tina, Lauren, Jesenia, Michael, Mary, Don, Renee, Andrea, Carlee, Yasemin, Erich, Nathalie, JJ, Ashlee, Kelsey, Ali, Leah, Michelle, Meghan. I have cried and ranted to you and asked for advice many times over the years and have been met with nothing but love, support, and understanding.

And to my NC friends: Elizabeth, Mike, Meredith,

Chesley, Kristin, Kathleen, Pierre, Jessica, Chase, and Erin, my day ones, my lifelongs. Thank you for always being interested in pretty much anything I have to say. It doesn't sound like much, but it means the world to me.

All the thanks to my manager, Lauren; my agents Melissa, Pamela, and Roberto; and the extended teams at Writ Large and Verve. Hopefully, I have given you both a new pilot and a screenplay by the time you're reading this! If not, I'm working on it!

To the extended Ezuma and Rankin families, Mama T, and Phanta, who have kept me in their prayers all these years. I love and appreciate you!

Thanks to Reading to Kids, a wonderful nonprofit I've had the pleasure of working with thirty-six Saturdays and counting. My experiences with y'all inspired Ndidi and Geoffrey's community outreach.

I'd like to shout out Juliet and Amanda of the *JAM Session* podcast. I'm a longtime listener, and your effusive praise of 831 Stories put this wonderful company on my radar!

And lastly, to the 831 Stories team, Erica, Claire, and Madi, for answering an unsolicited email and making my dream come true. Also, for connecting me to the delightful Sanjana Basker, whose insights and thoughtful commentary elevated the whole story. And to Jen Prokop not only for being a delightful editor who pushed me to make this story better but also for your podcast that has kept me entertained and thinking about the romance genre for years.

And if I forgot someone, I'm sorry! I'll get you in the next one (manifesting!)!!

ABOUT THE AUTHOR

TIFFANY EZUMA is a screenwriter and novelist who lives and writes in Los Angeles. She has a BA in political science and English from the University of North Carolina at Chapel Hill and an MFA in screenwriting from the University of Southern California. She does not have a cat, but if she did, this is where she would mention it.

If this left you wanting more...

did you know 831 Stories releases a book every month?

Sign up for The Ones:

A membership that gives you early access to every new 831 release—straight to your mailbox, e-reader, or audiobook player.

The Ones members also enjoy discounts across all of 831stories.com and special access to events, merch, and more.

Join or gift a membership today:

831STORIES.COM/THEONES

ALSO FROM 831 STORIES

Big Fan by Alexandra Romanoff

A high-profile scandal derailed Maya's DC career, and she's eager to fly under the radar—that is, until her former boy-band crush reaches out with a job offer.

Hardly Strangers by A.C. Robinson

One night with a rock star could upend Shera's best-laid plans, revealing how a chance encounter can rewrite a story—and change everything.

Comedic Timing by Upasna Barath

Naina is seeking a fresh start in NYC after breaking up with her girlfriend, but when she meets someone at a party, he's so offtype that her attraction to him fuels an identity crisis.

Set Piece by Lana Schwartz

When a breakout BBC star gets swarmed by fans during a night out, it's a no-nonsense bartender, CJ, who rescues him—and warms them both up for an after-hours hookup.

Square Waves by Alexandra Romanoff

The first spin-off in the *Big Fan* series, an enemies-to-lovers romance in which tabloid fodder mixes with a long-brewing rivalry as Cassidy contends with her high-school nemesis.

Exit Lane by Erika Veurink

A postcollege cross-country road trip sparks *something* between Marin and Teddy—though it's not quite clear what. Over the next eight years, they have fated encounters on multiple continents.

Grape Juice by Eliza Dumais

When Alice lands in France for a wine harvest, she's disenchanted with her life. But she soon finds something she's missing in the vineyard owner's nephew Henri, who's just as lost as she is.

Rooting Interest by Cat Disabato

When Felix gets pulled off her NFL beat to cover the WNBA, she doesn't expect to find herself so taken with the sport—or with one of its biggest stars, Natalie Czapski.

Found Time by Caroline Goldstein

Lili and Reid lock eyes after a 1993 Jeff Buckley show. Thirty years and a whole lifetime later, they cross paths once more. Can they finally make their way back to each other?

831 STORIES BOOK CREDITS

So many people were involved in bringing this book to life. Many of their names are included here, but there would be no HEA without the passionate work of booksellers and librarians and the enthusiasm of readers. And as we all know, romance readers are the best readers.

831 Stories

Erica Cerulo, Madison Feller, Marie Joh, Catherine Krenzer, Claire Mazur, Elaine Orihuela, Angela Vang

Authors Equity

Andrea Bachofen, Rose Edwards, Carly Gorga, Sarah Christensen Fu, Becca Kadison, Deb Lewis, Madeline McIntosh, Nina von Moltke, Diana Simmons, Erin Vandeveer, Don Weisberg, Craig Young

C47 Design

Phil Chang, Haneu Kang, Jamin Lee, Naomi Otsu, Sunny Park

831 STORIES BOOK CREDITS

Editing

Sanjana Basker, Meaghan O'Connell, Jen Prokop

Marketing, Events, and Publicity

Emma Benshoff, Zoë Gillespie, Tara Larsen, Ashleigh Magee, Kaitlin Phillips, Riley Vaske, Kristin White

Production

Sam Martin, Scribe Inc.

Keep reading for a taste of

Found Time

by Caroline Goldstein

from 831 Stories

I

"We're getting married," Nisha says as we walk to the Jeff Buckley show at Sin-é. I am uncomfortably aware of the crescent moons of sweat waxing at the armholes of my silk slip dress. This is the dumbest thing to wear in ninety-five-degree heat with one thousand percent humidity in the dead center of August, but I uncovered it at Screaming Mimi's for three dollars and made good on a promise to myself to wear things that look pretty but feel out of range. Trivial, sure, but maybe by taking small risks, I can somehow trick myself into becoming the person I want to be: free, embodied, and not so scared of the world. A little bit more like Nisha.

When I tried it on, I liked how the color of it, a sexy gunmetal gray, lifted the silver from my steel-blue eyes.

"I can't picture you in a wedding dress," I say now. I adjust my camera strap. It leaves a slick of sweat across my shoulder.

"That's because I won't be wearing a dress," Nisha responds. "I'll be wearing a bikini, as Jeff and I will be wed on the white-sand beaches of Bora Bora."

I laugh. "Your mother will be thrilled."

"She will be, actually. By that point, I will have discovered a cure for cancer, and that achievement will eclipse any questionable decisions I make thereafter."

"So we're going the biochemical engineering route today?"

Nisha grins. I don't know much about the singer-songwriter headlining tonight. But my best friend does. She's made it her mission to learn everything about him. He doesn't even have an album out but has already earned cult fame, in part through his appearances at the local spots—the Knitting Factory, Fez, Cornelia Street Café—and in part because he's the son of Tim Buckley, the folk-jazz musician who died of a heroin overdose at twenty-eight in 1975. Two years after Nisha and I were both born.

Nisha happened to sit next to Jeff at the SideWalk Cafe a couple of months ago, days after she and I moved into our apartment on Avenue A—a shoebox on the second floor of the building that also houses Two Boots, the pizza joint that effectively sustains us. And also, probably, the small colony of rats and cockroaches I once found peacefully coexisting underneath the warped floorboards of my bedroom.

When Nisha came home the afternoon of the Great Jeff Buckley Sighting, she told me that he drank his coffee black and smelled like cigarettes and peppers and rose soap.

She was sure she had fallen in love. Not that she worked up the courage to talk to him. He had the aura of an immortal, and she was merely a rising junior at NYU who didn't even know whether she wanted to major in biochemical engineering or physics.

As we round the corner onto St. Mark's, I accidentally kick a syringe. I watch it clatter into the street, where it's promptly run over by a bike messenger. No amount of NYPD officers, glossy condos, or newly opened Gap stores can buff the East Village to a shine.

We reach Sin-é, and my pace slows when I notice a limousine parked in front. A tendril of cigarette smoke curls out the driver's side window.

"I think your husband's going to be famous." I gesture to the car. It's so slick, just begging to be broken into. Only record-label people would be so arrogant as to bring it down here.

Nisha shrugs. "You don't think talented people deserve success?"

"Of course I do. I just don't think talented people need to sell out to do it."

She opens the café door for me. "Oh, my sweet, sheltered Lili. If only we could all be gifted artists with artistic parents. Life would be so much simpler."

"Simpler, maybe. But I'll never be able to afford the lavish lifestyle I truly crave," I joke. We both know I would happily subsist on cans of chickpeas for the rest of my life if it meant I could keep doing photography.

I gently push my way toward the stage, which is really just a few square feet of floor with a banner reading "Sin-é" hanging on the wall above it. Two years ago, I would have been trailing Nisha, but I'm trying to be bolder. Since the moment she came blazing into my room to introduce herself on move-in day of our freshman year, I knew I needed her kind of energy in my life. She was already glimmering then, and tonight, she is incandescent in her silver-foil minidress with a hot-pink bindi gleaming between her brows.

I've been to Sin-é once or twice, but never when the narrow, brick-walled room has been so full. It's mostly fellow NYU students, moonlighting actors, and some grizzled old Irish men, but over in the corner, at the table closest to the door, I spot two people, maybe in their midtwenties, locked in a conversation. Their heads are bowed over their steaming mugs—they famously don't serve hard liquor here, only tea, coffee, and cans of Rolling Rock—and the woman has a blood-red buzzcut and a slash of lipstick to match. She looks like a regular.

But the man is clean-cut, clad in a full suit despite the heat. Conspicuous among this sea of denim and facial hair. When he picks up his coffee cup, his watch flashes. He looks like a limousine rider.

All the tables are taken, the walls already lined with spectators, so Nisha and I have no choice but to sit on the floor, right in front of this duo. I shudder to think of dry-cleaning my dress, which will likely cost three times as much as the actual garment.

The toe of the man's dress shoe nudges my butt cheek. I feel my face burn. He quickly retracts his foot.

"Sorry," he mumbles. I pick up his scent, distinct even over the aroma of spilled beer that's soaked into the floorboards. Something piney. A sharp contrast to the sweltering day.

Nisha taps my knee and gestures to the stage. Jeff Buckley has appeared underneath the banner, his white Telecaster hanging across his chest. He's probably just come out of the bathroom, but it's like he conjured himself into being.

Now I understand what Nisha has been banging on about these past few months. This guy *glows*.

He steps in front of the mic and slings his guitar behind his back. He stomps his boot on the floor in a rhythmic beat. To someone offstage, he says, "Oh, you're rolling. Goodness. Is there any reverb to roll with?"

Then he begins punctuating his stomps with claps, and the song takes shape: Nina Simone's "Be My Husband." Nisha squeezes my knee in silent alarm. This is her favorite song, from her favorite Nina Simone album. This, the squeeze implies, is fate at work.

Jeff pulls his guitar around to play the second song, something I have never heard before but which evokes a familiar emotion: the irresistible melancholy of longing. Encountering this kind of sublimity is so overwhelming that it makes me want to capture it in an image. Discreetly, I take a single photo, the *click* of the shutter buried in the reverb. Then I abandon the camera and give myself over entirely to the moment. Over the course of the set, Jeff sometimes leans against the wall, like he's fiddling around in his own living room, casually being a genius. Sometimes he cradles his guitar closer to his chest, turning its face up so he can gaze upon it with more attention, as if it were a lover.

When the set ends, I look over at Nisha. Her face is streaked with tears.

"I think I just saw god," Nisha says.

For once—and just this once—Nisha is not overreacting.

"Go talk to him," I urge her. "Do it now, before he gets too famous."

At the front of the room, Jeff is already being swallowed up by the crowd. Nisha moves, zombie-like, into the fray.

I peel myself off the ground, unsticking my dress from the unswept floor. When I stand, my knees buckle underneath me. My legs have fallen asleep. *How much time just passed?*

"What'd you think?"

The guy in the suit. Over the past however long, I had been so fixated on the music, and the musician, that I'd almost forgotten he was just above me.

Earlier, I could tell that he was handsome, if out of place. Now I see that he's unbearably hot—and also, somehow, intensely familiar. As if I've previously seen the way his forearms flex under his rolled-up shirtsleeves, and already know how a section of his dark hair falls, curling over one eye. Like I'm familiar with how the corners of his mouth turn downward, not up, when he smiles, which makes it seem like he's harboring a secret I'm desperate to be in on. As though I've already heard the deep rumble of his laugh. And felt the weight of his body pressing me up against a wall.

It doesn't make sense. But to question it—I don't know where to start.

"I thought . . . I don't know what I thought," I say. "I have nothing to compare it to."

"In a good way or a bad way?" he asks.

For a moment, I wonder if I have the future of Jeff Buckley's career in my hands. "Definitely in a good way. I don't think he's signed yet, but if he's not, he should be."

"I agree."

I shift on my feet, still trying to get the blood moving in my legs. I touch the back of the man's chair for balance, accidentally brushing against his suit jacket, which he's folded and neatly draped over the back. His eyes shift to my fingers, then trail up my arm, my shoulder, my neck. I force myself to blink.

He nods at the red-haired girl. "You ready to go, Cat?"

"What time is it?" Cat runs her hand over her head.

He checks his watch. Up close, I see that it's a scuffed Timex. Not fancy after all. "Seven fifteen."

"Dinner's not until eight. Dad can wait."

Dad. My gaze darts between them.

"The express is running local," the guy says. "It'll takc an hour to get up to Park."

"So you don't havc a limo," I start. When they look at me blankly, I add, "So you can whisk Jeff Buckley away and offer him a million-dollar record deal? With a golden tablespoon of coke as a signing bonus?"

Cat cackles and elbows the guy. "I told you, you look like a fucking suit."

"Well, I am one, for the summer."

"Not record-label people, then." I feel foolish, out of sorts.

I look out the window. The limo is gone. So are the musician and his gear, I discover as I glance around the room. Patrons are slowly making their way out to the street, into the hot, real world.

I feel a flicker of panic. I'm not ready to go back out there. I'm not ready to face the impending school year—or the fact that I desperately need to get a job this semester after spending the summer doing nothing other than sunning myself in Tompkins Square Park and sneaking photographs of the leftover eighties punks, their mohawks drooping in the heat. I'm not ready to replace the feelings this night elicited with the avalanche of things I need to do.

"I'm definitely not cool enough to be a record-label person," the man says. "I have a temp gig at my uncle's investment firm."

"Which means he's basically working for free," Cat cuts in.

"I'm making enough to get myself this suit." He brushes his hands down his pant legs.

"My point exactly," Cat says. "Ten dollars an hour, Reid. I'd make more as a waitress at Veselka."

Reid. So the man has a name. A good one too.

"You're a waitress at Veselka?" I ask. If so, it would be a little like encountering East Village royalty.

"No." Cat smirks. "But I did fuck a line cook one time."

Reid laughs, then he turns back to me, his eyes studying

something. I'm suddenly very aware that I'm not wearing a bra, and that the hard peaks of my nipples are likely making this obvious to him as well.

He clears his throat. "I like your camera."

I fiddle with the strap. "Are you into photography?"

"Looking at it, sure. But I can't be the one doing it, assuming you want your head in the photo."

I try to fight a smile.

"Reid does write screenplays in secret, though. And they're actually not terrible." Cat arches her brows. I give Reid a glance that says, *Really?* and he returns one that says, *Up for debate.* "Which makes it even more of a shame that my dad has him identifying acquisition targets for IBM."

"I'm not actually identifying acquisition targets," Reid says to me, as if I know what those words mean. "I'm making photocopies and binding books out of research that other people did about identifying acquisition targets."

"Yes, but what beautiful binding skills you have." Cat grabs his chin between her thumb and her forefinger, giving it a squeeze. "My dad is no less immune to this *punim* than those girls are."

She motions to the table behind them. The two women sitting there look away quickly, caught.

"They've been staring at you this entire time," Cat stage-whispers.

Inexplicably, I feel a flare of jealousy.

That's when Nisha reappears, announcing her return with a forceful "*Lili!*" Her usual entrance.

"Did you get to talk to him?" I scan her face.

"He left with some people from Columbia Records," Nisha says. I exchange inside-joke glances with Cat and Reid. Reid's gaze lingers on mine.

"But guess what I got?" Nisha asks.

"His panties?" Cat quips.

"Almost better." Nisha waves a crumpled napkin in front of my face. "The address of someone who knows Jeff Buckley's manager. Apparently the manager is having a party right now, and this girl said Jeff might come later. We're going." She cocks her head, addressing Cat and Reid. "You guys could come, if you want to."

I'm not surprised by Nisha's invitation—this is not the first time my ever-magnanimous friend has encouraged strangers to tag along with us. Or the first time that a stranger has been a hot guy who I'm too shy to ask out myself.

"We have to go to dinner at my uncle's apartment." Reid looks at me like this warrants an apology. "I owe him . . . well, a lot. But at the very least showing up for dinner at his apartment."

Before I can consider a response, Cat is shaking her head. Her stack of silver earrings clacks vigorously. "One does not just *pass up* an opportunity to party with *Jeff Buckley*. Let me call my dad and get us out of it." She turns to Nisha. "Where is this thing?"

"520 East Fifth."

Cat claps her hands together once. "I'll use the pay phone on Sixth. We're good to go. *Allons-y*."

Already Cat and Nisha are halfway out the door. Reid

is frozen in place on his stool, and I watch his face closely, attempting to read whatever he's thinking.

He smiles, then stands. He's taller than I would have thought. Towering. "I'll come for thirty minutes, then I'll head uptown."

"Sure," I say, like we both already know this bit. Like it's a regular game we play.

His eyes soften when he looks down at me; it's as if I've elicited that response in him a thousand times before, and now I am simply remembering it.

Then I feel a falling sensation in my stomach. A plummet.

That is new.

"Lili," he says, and I can't even remember whatever Jeff Buckley just did with his magic hands and his enchanted tongue—my name in Reid's mouth is the most beautiful thing I have ever heard. I would do anything to make him say it again.

"Reid," I respond.

That downturned smile. "Let's see what's happening on Fifth Street."